# FORGOTTEN

# FORGOTTEN

## Seventeen and Homeless

## Melody Carlson

NAVPRESS

Discipleship Inside Out™

THiNK

**NAVPRESS**
Discipleship Inside Out™

NavPress is the publishing ministry of The Navigators, an international Christian organization and leader in personal spiritual development. NavPress is committed to helping people grow spiritually and enjoy lives of meaning and hope through personal and group resources that are biblically rooted, culturally relevant, and highly practical.

**For a free catalog go to www.NavPress.com**
**or call 1.800.366.7788 in the United States or 1.800.839.4769 in Canada.**

ISBN-13: 978-1-60006-948-2

Cover design by The DesignWorks Group, Charles Brock
Cover image by John Bailey, Shutterstock

Published in association with the literary agency of Sara A. Fortenberry.

Some of the anecdotal illustrations in this book are true to life and are included with the permission of the persons involved. All other illustrations are composites of real situations, and any resemblance to people living or dead is coincidental.

Library of Congress Cataloging-in-Publication Data

Carlson, Melody.
  Forgotten : a novel / Melody Carlson.
    p. cm.
  Summary: With the rent overdue and her bipolar mother missing, seventeen-year-old Adele is forced out of her home and although she tries to maintain the pretense of normality, things rapidly fall apart.
  ISBN 978-1-60006-948-2 (alk. paper)
  [1. Homeless persons--Fiction. 2. Christian life--Fiction. 3. High school--Fiction. 4. Schools--Fiction.] I. Title.
  PZ7.C216637For 2010
  [Fic]--dc22

2010013317

Printed in the United States of America

1 2 3 4 5 6 7 8 / 14 13 12 11 10

I allowed myself to believe there was such a thing as do-overs a few months ago. I should've known better, but it was a hot July afternoon and my head was throbbing after a torturous day of selling hot dogs from a greasy, smelly food kiosk owned by a "friend" of my mom's.

Vernon (aka "Vermin") Smithers had worked a deal with someone in the city, allowing him to park his Hot Diggity Dog House right in front of the town's only public swimming pool, which meant I worked like a dog, sweated like a pig, and never got a break or a tip. I was subjected to this inhumane treatment for the miserly reward of minimum wage. To top it all off, at the end of my shift, feeling and smelling like an overcooked hot dog myself, I had to ride my bike home.

Consequently, on that day when my mom announced that life as I knew it was about to change, I barely even questioned her. "I'm taking a job in Stanfield," she blurted out as soon as I opened the front door.

"Stanfield . . ." I went for the fridge, scavenging to find a cold soda. "Isn't that like a couple hundred miles from here?"

"I already gave notice on our house," she said in an excited voice. "We have to be out of here by the end of the month. My job starts the first week of August."

"Seriously?" I wiped the cold can across my throbbing forehead and attempted to think rationally. Heat stroke or not, this was my life we were talking about. Well, my mom's and mine. Still, I wasn't sure how to react. I mean, as much as I loved my mom, she'd never been the most reliable, predictable, or dependable person on the planet. Plus, she's bipolar, and judging by the gleam in her bright blue eyes, she was definitely experiencing a high that day.

"I know exactly what you're thinking, Adele." Her brow creased as she pressed her lips tightly together. "But this time you're wrong."

I decided to play innocent as I sat on the futon that also served as my bed. "I'm not thinking anything, Mom. I'm just surprised about this new development. Tell me what's going on."

Her smile returned. "Well, it's a huge opportunity for me — for both of us. In fact, you'll get to graduate from a school that's rated really high in the state." Then she rattled on, telling me more pluses and perks about Stanfield as well as the old college friend who offered the job to her. "I have no doubt that this move is exactly what we both need, Adele."

It was clear she'd done some research too. And although I felt a twinge of doubt because . . . well, I know my mom . . . and I know she exaggerates sometimes . . . and I know she has her "issues." Despite all that, I was getting onboard with this idea.

No doubt, I was weak and vulnerable, but the possibility of quitting my nasty summer job enticed me. And I had no problem with switching schools either. My junior year had been a huge disappointment. And as for close friends, I didn't have any. As pathetic as it sounded, there was no one I'd regret leaving behind.

My mom was flying high as she went on and on about how great this would be. "This is the fresh start we both desperately need. We'll both enjoy a new and improved life."

And the more I listened to her, the more I bought into the whole thing. In fact, I didn't protest a bit. I was in. And really, it was about time our luck changed. According to my mom, her ship had finally come in and we were both getting on it and sailing away.

So I gave Vernon notice on my job, and two weeks later, I was packing boxes. I even scrubbed and scoured our tiny apartment in hopes of getting our deposit back (which never happened). But as I worked, I imagined my mom and me in our new life. Everything would be all fresh and squeaky clean there — kind of like a Febreze commercial where everything came out smelling sweet.

"Get rid of anything you don't like," Mom told me as I was packing up my room. "As soon as we get to Stanfield, we'll go on a major shopping spree and get all new stuff. And then before I start my new job, we'll both get makeovers and new wardrobes and some cool furnishings for the condo. Everything new!"

"We can afford this, right?" I ventured once more — kind of like a reality check. I mean, really, sometimes it all just seemed too good to be true.

"I already explained everything to you, Adele." Her voice took on the sharp edge of impatience. "Mark Edmonds gave me that advance on my salary to help us relocate. He set up the condo for us. We're covered. Don't be such a worrywart. Sometimes you're like an old woman!"

I nodded and returned to packing. I had actually seen the check her new boss sent — and the amount was impressive. I also went with my mom as she deposited it in the bank. And I was even more impressed when I later discovered the check had cleared at the bank. Thanks to my mom's "challenges," I know all about online banking, how to pay bills, and how to tuck away a bit of money for a rainy day. My life's been filled with a lot of those.

So knowing that the money was in the bank and my mom's job was for real, I felt seriously hopeful. And why not? My mom had a good education; she was intelligent and capable of holding down a good job. Not that it had happened for the past several years. But that could change. My mom's problems had gotten worse after my deadbeat dad walked out. But that was more than six years ago. She was probably over it.

My mom's job skills were "valuable" — and I'd heard many times about how she could easily bring home a six-figure salary when the economy turned around. A couple of times she did get hired, but then something would happen . . . and it would unravel. But there was unemployment . . . and other things. However, I wasn't going there. This time life would be different. And it was different . . . at first anyway.

"This place looks fabulous," I told my mom as she pulled into Westwood Heights, a pleasantly arranged complex of three-story buildings nestled into some attractive landscaping, including lots of tall oak trees. Before long we were hauling boxes into our second-floor unit, which was even better than the exterior. With an open floor plan, high ceilings, a gas fireplace, and a stylish kitchen complete with granite and stainless steel, it was a huge improvement over our previous digs. But the best part was the two master suites. Not only did I have a real bedroom now, but I actually had my own bathroom as well!

Then, true to her word, Mom took us shopping the next week. I felt like a princess as I splurged at stores like Banana

Republic and Gap, buying the kinds of clothes I used to just dream about.

It was late July, and I couldn't wait for the first day of school to come. I could imagine myself walking in with my head held high—pretending I was someone else. And from now on I would use my full name. No more being called "Addie." I was *Adele* Porter and my senior year was going to rock! It would be totally unlike my previous year, where I went around like a meek little mouse, hoping no one would notice my thrift-store jeans and worn-out shoes. This would be my year to shine. I would join clubs and start planning for college. And I might even make some real friends.

At least that's what I tell myself as I ride the transit to Stanfield High on registration day the week before school starts. And whether it's the power of positive thinking or just plain luck, it seems to be working.

"Hey, you're new." A blonde girl steps behind me in the line for twelfth grade. She's wearing a pale denim skirt topped with a pink T-shirt. She's pretty but not flashy, more of a wholesome kind of pretty. And she has a nice smile.

"Yeah. We just moved here last month." I suppress the urge to nervously smooth the front of my shirt. After trying several outfits, I decided on this fitted white button-up I'd gotten at Express. "Understated but classic," the salesgirl assured me. I'd paired this with what were supposedly "the coolest jeans this side of the Mississippi," some killer Nine West sandals, and a knockoff Prada bag my mom thought was convincing. To say I felt like a million bucks as I walked from the bus stop to the school would not have been an understatement. But for some reason, standing in front of this girl who looks very comfortable in her own skin, I feel totally out of my league and a bit like a counterfeit. Like I'm as genuine as my fake Prada purse.

"Cool bag." She lowers her voice in a confidential tone. "Prada, right? Is it the *real* deal?"

I'm not sure how to respond but decide to go with honesty since it's usually the safest route. "Are you kidding?" I force what I hope looks like a confident smile. "Why waste good money on something that'll be out of style by Christmas?"

She laughs loudly. "Exactamundo!"

I almost comment on her odd choice of expressions, but stop myself and simply nod. No sense in alienating anyone — especially when I'm still the new girl here.

She sticks out her hand. "I'm Isabella Marx, senior class president."

I cock my head to one side. "You mean you've already had student body elections?"

She shrugs in a slightly sheepish way. "Okay, that's just an assumption on my part. But I was freshman, sophomore, and junior class president . . . so I suppose it seems likely I'll win it again."

"Wow, that's impressive."

"And one responsibility of being class president is welcoming new students. So consider yourself officially welcomed. Uh, what did you say your name was?"

"I didn't." I smile. "I'm Adele Porter."

"Welcome to Stanfield High, Adele Porter." And then to my surprise, Isabella kind of takes me under her wing. First she introduces me to a couple of the faculty helping with registration, then she helps me get a good schedule of classes, and finally, she even gives me a quick tour of the campus. "This way you won't have first-day-of-school nightmares about not being able to find your locker." She chuckles.

I blink. "Do you have those too?"

"Not since before my freshman year."

It seems the tour is done now. So I thank Isabella for her time and am ready to make what I hope will be a graceful exit and head back to the bus stop, but she stops me.

"You need to come meet some people." She leads me over to where a small group of kids are drinking sodas in a shady area of the courtyard, and just like that, she introduces me to her friends. I feel almost like I'm dreaming as these kids chat openly and naturally with me, like it's no big deal or they've known me for years. It's pretty surreal.

"Adele is into journalism," Isabella informs a petite redhead named Lily Bishop.

"Me too." Lily tells me what classes she has, and I pull out my schedule to discover we both have journalism the same period.

Then a tall guy named Ethan Daniels looks over my shoulder. "Hey, you're in calculus with me."

"And if you need any help, Ethan's your man," Isabella says. Then she introduces me to a guy I swear looks just like Jude Law. "This is Jayden Hammaker."

Jayden points to the schedule still in my hand. "It looks like we have resource together."

"What is that anyway?" I ask.

"Your free period," Isabella says.

"You have to check in," Jayden informs me, "but then you can go to the library or whatever."

"Right." I nod like none of this is the slightest bit over-whelming to me . . . like this is totally normal . . . like I am used to fitting in. But am I in shock? Maybe some kind of culture shock? I remember reading about this once. But something about being received like this, feeling genuinely welcomed by kids I've never even met before . . . well, it's all pretty weird. But also cool. And I like it.

As I ride the transit home, I feel strangely hopeful. Like all the things I've been imagining for the upcoming year are really going to come true . . . like this is going to be a life-changing year, after all. And so far, my mom seems happy with her new life, too. It's only been a little more than three weeks, and although some of her earlier enthusiasm has worn off, she's still talking positively about her job. So, really, why should I be worried?

## CHAPTER 2

School starts the day after Labor Day, and within that first week, I figure out two very significant things about Isabella and her friends. First of all, although they aren't in the snootiest clique at SHS, which is a relief, they are still relatively high up in the high school feeding chain. As a result, they are somewhat exclusive — a tad bit snobby even. I get the impression they come from fairly well-off families — kind of the who's who of Stanfield. Although they play it down.

The second thing I discover is that Isabella and her friends are quite academic . . . a bit more intellectual, or so they assume, than the rest of the student body. And talk of college scholarships and SAT scores isn't uncommon at their lunchroom table. Yes, they have their own table. No one seems to dispute this either. Anyway, although they are academic, it's not like they talk incessantly about education, which would be lame. But they're not afraid to discuss whatever comes up . . . from politics to books to maintaining a GPA and precollege courses.

Oddly enough, I'm able to hold my own with them. Thanks to my mom's new job (at what seems to be a prestigious marketing firm — and it helps that Lily's dad works there too) and my own scholastic background, which is relatively strong, I can almost appear to be one of them. Sure, I still feel a bit like an imposter, but I can get past this. And by the second week of school, I actually feel like I am becoming one of them. And it feels awesome.

"I'm pretty sure I'm going to get an early acceptance from Yale," Bristol Allen announces to the group on Friday. Bristol and Isabella have been on and off best friends since grade school. Lily confided this much to me in journalism the other day, letting it slip that there'd been a love triangle last spring. Jayden Hammaker had been in the center with both Isabella and Bristol fighting for his affection. "Not that it worked," Lily told me. "Jayden was so not interested." Anyway, it seems that Bristol and Isabella have moved on since they're relatively civilized to each other. Plus, I'm guessing that Isabella has her eye on Ethan now, and I'm guessing that Ethan feels the same.

Jayden is peering at Bristol with a skeptical expression now. "You honestly think you'll get an early acceptance from *Yale?*"

She nods a bit smugly. "I expect to hear something from them before Christmas."

"Don't hold your breath, Bristol." Isabella smirks as she sticks a straw in her soda. "Yale's a long shot, for you anyway."

Bristol's dark eyes flash. "How would you even know? It's not like you're applying to any *Ivy League* schools."

"That's because I'm going to my parents' alma mater." Isabella makes a face at Bristol. "Which some people happen to think is preferable to any of the *Ivy League* schools."

"And most Ivy League schools don't do early acceptance," Jayden informs her.

Bristol holds her head high. "FYI . . . one of my dad's best friends happens to be on the Yale admissions board."

Jayden just shakes his head. "Trust me, Bristol, it'll take

more than a buddy on the board to get an early acceptance from Yale. That is, unless you're someone they really want. Some hot commodity they don't want to miss out on." His eyes twinkle like he knows this isn't the situation.

"Or maybe you have some hidden talents we don't know about," Lily teases.

Bristol scowls and looks like she's about to argue this when Ethan changes the subject. "So, who's going to the big game tonight? It's supposed to be a good one." The response from the table is less than enthusiastic, and I can tell Ethan's disappointed. Even so, I don't say anything to encourage him. The truth is, I like sports, but I'm guessing this clique's not into the whole jock thing — and I'm not comfortable enough to rock the boat.

Isabella looks at Ethan. "Well, I'd like to go to the game."

"Cool." He nods eagerly. "How about I give you a ride?"

And just like that, it all turns around. Everyone starts acting like they want to go too. Suddenly they're planning rides, Lily offers to get there early to save seats, and some of them are arguing on where to eat afterward. I can't help but be impressed at Isabella's influence with this crowd, yet she seems to simply take it in stride. To my relief, she's including me in these plans too. "Who are you riding with?"

Before I can object, Ethan decides that I must ride with Isabella and him. I have a feeling it's because Bristol was trying to squeeze herself in. Maybe there's still a rift between those two girls. Now as much as I appreciate being included, I'm a little concerned that Ethan's the one offering the ride. I do not want Isabella to perceive this as me trying to push into whatever may or may not be going on between Ethan and her. No way do I want to blow my friendship with her — especially after only two weeks as the "new girl."

"How about if I hitch a ride with you, too?" Jayden suggests to Ethan. "That way we'll save on gas."

Ethan agrees, and as quickly as they came, my fears fade away. Not only am I being included in this group, but I'm going on what almost seems like a double date! Okay, it's not like I'm delusional; I know Jayden hasn't asked me out proper, but I must admit it feels extremely cool to imagine it that way. I've never been on a real date. Last year I thought a guy was going to ask me out. But a girl who I had supposed was my friend told him my mom was crazy, and that kind of squelched the date — not to mention the rest of my junior year. But that's an old story.

Anyway, I am still riding high when I get home from school on Friday. So high that I don't really stop to wonder why my mom came home from work early. My focus is on putting together the coolest outfit I can for the football game. Something that will encourage Jayden to give me a second look. Or so I hope.

It's not until Isabella calls me on my cell phone, announcing that Ethan has just turned into my condo complex and that I'm supposed to meet them down there, that I notice my mom's grim expression. She's seated on the couch with her arms folded tightly across her chest like something is really bugging her.

"Is something wrong?" I ask as I pull on my jacket.

She scowls darkly. It's a look I haven't seen in months, but it sends chills through me. "Just my ridiculous excuse of a boss," she snaps. "*That's all.*"

"Something's wrong at work?" I feel uneasy as I reach for my bag.

She stands then, rolling her eyes dramatically. "Nothing I can't manage, Adele. Don't bother yourself to worry about me or my problems. You just run along with your little friends.

*Have fun!*" The mocking tone of her voice is laced with anger now. And although I know that whatever's going on isn't really my fault, I feel guilty. My mom will find a way to blame me for this. She always does.

I just kind of nod then, mumbling something that I hope sounds sympathetic as I rush out the door. But that tone in her voice . . . that look in her eyes . . . it's all too familiar. And it is not a good sign. My mom's world is starting to unravel again. Already—it's falling apart!

But as I hurry down the stairs, I do not want to think about that. I do not want my mom's problems to ruin what's going on in my world. I am simply imagining things. And sure, maybe something is wrong, but like my mom said, she will manage it. She will put it back together. After all, that's what parents are supposed to do. And it's about time my mom accepted this and got on with it.

I hear a honk from the other side of the parking lot and hurry over to where Ethan's car is parked near the street. Isabella said to look for a small silver car. I'm not sure what the make is, but I can see it's fairly new and I suspect it's one of the new hybrid designs.

"Cool car," I tell Ethan as I slide into the backseat where Jayden is already seated.

"Thanks." Ethan turns and grins. "Gets almost forty miles per gallon on the highway."

"Sweet."

"So, how long have you lived in Westwood Heights?" Jayden asks me as Ethan pulls out into the street.

"Just since summer. The condo kind of came with my mom's job. But we'll probably move into something a little nicer in a while." Okay, even as those words spew from my mouth, it's like I have no idea where they originated. Who do I think I'll impress with that stupid lie? And why? Anyway, it's too late.

"There's a house for sale next door to us," Isabella says. "You should tell your mom to come by and check it out. If she bought it, we'd be neighbors."

"That'd be cool." I grimace inwardly.

Jayden gives me a slightly questioning look, as if he knows more about my situation than I thought. But he doesn't say anything. And again I must be imagining things. Really, there's no way Jayden or anyone else at my school could possibly know anything besides what I've let out—and that hasn't been much. And it will be even less from now on. For sure, there will be no more spinning little "white" lies either. I know from years of watching my mom's mistakes what kind of trouble deceitfulness brings. Not that I want to think about any of that tonight.

After Ethan parks near the football stadium, he and Isabella walk together (actually holding hands, which makes me think their relationship is moving right along). Jayden probably feels like he should follow suit, so we walk side by side too—although no hand holding is involved. And even though I know we aren't really on a date, I pretend we are. Once we're inside the stadium, I allow the charade to continue by sitting next to him. Not that he seems to mind—if anything, it feels expected. Or else I'm just feeling hopeful.

But during the first half, I can't help but notice Bristol. She and Lily are sitting on the bleacher in front of us, and every once in a while, Bristol glances back with an expression that feels kind of like jealousy. Unless I'm imagining it. And that's possible since Bristol was crushing on Jayden last year. Anyway, that's what I try to convince myself—that Bristol's jealousy is just my imagination. Or maybe she's just curious.

I must admit it feels intriguing to be the girl of interest. To be in an "enviable" position. I mean, it's so unlike my previous life. Just the same, it's unsettling. I'm fully aware that I'm still the new girl here, and I can't afford to make any enemies at SHS. So at halftime I make some lame excuse to Jayden, saying I want to talk to Lily, who's sitting next to Bristol. I sit by Lily and make small talk with them about the game, acting totally nonchalant, like I have no idea Bristol may have been shooting dagger looks in my direction.

"Are you sitting with us for the rest of the game?" Bristol asks me in a slightly irritated tone, like maybe this spot on the bleacher is reserved for someone more important than me.

"Is that okay?" I watch her closely as a somewhat catty smile appears.

"Absolutely. In fact, I'll go grab your seat before anyone else gets it." And just like that, she's sitting next to Jayden. Since he doesn't glance back at me or act the least bit concerned, I figure it's probably for the best. I mean, Jayden's a cool guy, and if I were a different person (someone more secure and not freaking out over every little thing), it might be fun to have someone like Jayden interested in me. In other words . . . *in my dreams!*

As I sit there in the cool autumn night air, pretending to be focused on the game that our team appears to be winning, I am totally distracted. Despite my resolve to block it out, I can't stop thinking about my mom's gloomy mood tonight. How long will it be until this lovely little life I've barely started to build begins to crumble and fall apart? And if this whole thing is going to disintegrate anyway, why should I even go to the trouble to create it in the first place? Seriously, I could do without this stress.

With only a couple minutes left in the game, I realize our team is down by six points, and I am still obsessing over my mom. Worst-case scenario, my mom will lose her job, collect some unemployment, and I'll have to find some part-time work to help ends meet. Naturally, it will be the end of my short-lived social life. We'll have to move to some cheap housing and, consequently, I'll need to disappear from this crowd. But hopefully I'll get to finish high school . . . and get a scholarship . . . and go away to college next fall. Really, I wouldn't be that much worse off from my previous school. And someday this will all be over and I will be on my own. Because I've seen enough to know that until I'm on my own, I will always be pulled under . . . whenever my mom gets pulled under. That's just the way it works with us.

Suddenly the game is over and our team made a comeback, winning by one point! Everyone is cheering and jumping and hugging. And to my surprise, Jayden grabs me and hugs me tightly—and I hug him back.

"Did I do something to offend you?" he asks me while we're still embracing.

"No, of course not," I say as he releases me from his arms.

"But you switched seats."

My cheeks flush as a thrill rushes through me. "I didn't think you'd even notice."

He frowns. "I noticed."

"I'm sorry." Just then I glance over to see Bristol nearby. She's pretending not to be watching us as she chats with Isabella, but I can tell what she's really focused on.

"I just didn't want to rock anyone's boat," I explain to Jayden. "You know what I mean?"

His frown fades. "Yeah, I think I do know. So, are you still coming with us for pizza?"

"If you want me—"

"Don't be ridiculous." He links his arm in mine and leads

me down the bleacher steps. "I'm starving, people," he calls out over his shoulder. "Let's get this show on the road."

And just like that, the rest of our group follows. As we trek through the parking lot, I try not to think about Bristol, but I can hear her and Lily talking behind us. Then Lily yells over to another friend, a guy I barely know named Caleb, offering him a ride and asking him if he wants to go have pizza too. So that means Bristol will be there as well. Not that there's much I can do about it one way or the other.

Once we're back in Ethan's car, Jayden looks curiously at me. "Is something bugging you?"

I shrug. "Not really . . ."

"Hey, don't let Bristol get to you," Isabella says from the front seat.

"What . . . uh . . . do you mean?"

Isabella throws back her head and laughs. "Right, Adele. Don't tell me you don't know what's going on with Bristol. I know you're not stupid."

I let out a loud sigh. "Okay, Lily told me that Bristol was kind of into Jayden last year. But I guess I thought it was over with."

"That shows how well you know Bristol." Ethan starts his car.

"Anyway, I get the feeling she's not too happy with me right now," I admit.

"Not too happy?" Isabella chuckles. "That's putting it mildly."

"Great." I groan. "Are you guys trying to tell me that just two weeks into the school year, I've made a serious enemy?"

"Be flattered." Isabella turns to peer at me. "Bristol wouldn't waste her jealousy on you if she didn't think you were worth it."

Now Jayden laughs. "Don't worry, Adele. Bristol is mostly harmless."

"*Mostly* harmless?" I eye him in the dimly lit backseat.

"Just a little backstabbing here . . . a drop of poison there . . . a bit of Facebook scamming," Ethan says dramatically. "It wasn't too bad, was it, Isabella?"

She lets out a hoot of laughter. "Not if you're tough."

I lean back in the seat and actually giggle. The mere fact that we're even having this conversation has left me a bit light-headed. Does this mean that Jayden is seriously interested in me? And if he is, how do I feel? Besides elated, that is?

"Actually, I *am* pretty tough." No way will I ever admit to what's toughened me up over the years, but it's the truth — I am tough. At least I thought I was . . .

Jayden slaps my knee and nods. "Good for you, Adele Porter. Because I could use a *tough* woman by my side."

Okay, I have to laugh at that. Whether it's my frazzled nerves, the anticipation of romance, or just plain humor, I let myself go and laugh hard. We all do. And it feels incredibly good to just cut loose and be silly like this. I'm sure I needed it.

But then I think seriously about my situation. Why should I let some spoiled brat like Bristol get the best of me? Good grief, I have much bigger worries to freak over. In fact, my larger problems (aka my mom's problems) could soon put an end to my social life anyway. And if it's not going to last long, why not enjoy it while I have the chance? So in that moment I decide that Bristol or no Bristol, I am going to have as much fun as I possibly can before the roof caves in on me.

Because it will cave in . . . eventually. It always does.

To my surprise and relief, week three of my "new life" is going exceptionally well. At least on the surface. And that's all I'm focusing on these days. *The surface*. Does that make me shallow? Maybe, but maybe I don't care.

The good news is that my mom seems to be going to work every day. I mean, she gets up and gets dressed, and she might be running late or coming home early, but at least she's still getting up and going. That in itself has been part of the battle in her previous jobs. So it still looks fairly good — on the surface. Beneath that . . . well, it's anyone's guess.

But I'm not guessing. I just keep saying positive things to her, telling her that she's so smart and talented and how she's probably really great at work, flattering her about how fantastic she looks, asking if she's lost weight — whatever it takes to keep her going. I need her to keep going. And basically I will say anything I can think of to keep encouraging her. Because I'm still hoping that this time will be different for us. And if I don't think too hard, I can almost make myself believe it.

On the school front, I am fairly certain Jayden really likes me. But we're still at the flirting stage, which is actually kind of fun. And it's especially nice for me since this whole dating thing is pretty new. I'm not in any hurry. Although Isabella keeps assuming Jayden and I are a real couple, I keep telling her it's too soon to say. Fortunately, she's so into Ethan that there doesn't seem to be any jealousy factor with her. Apparently her interest in Jayden ended last summer. I wish I could say the same about Bristol. Because that girl is making my life miserable. I try very hard not to show it, and I seriously do not want her to hate me. I don't think I can afford it. But today in art, it takes every ounce of my self-control not to smack her.

"Your mouth looks nothing like that." She stands over my shoulder looking at what is supposed to be a self-portrait.

I just shrug and focus on the lower lip I'm sketching. And okay, I may have made the mouth a little too big, but I've always been told I have "full lips."

"Mr. Klein told us to *exaggerate* our facial features," Lindsey, the girl who shares a table with Bristol and me, quietly says. "See how I made my hair a lot fuller than it really is?"

I compare her straight shoulder-length black hair to the drawing and think it looks almost identical. Although the eyes in the drawing are much more dramatic and exotic than her serious gray eyes. Maybe that's wishful drawing on her part.

"Was anyone talking to you?" Bristol glares at Lindsey.

I give Lindsey a wimpy smile and wish I had the nerve to say something more. She seems like a nice girl, but for some reason Bristol seems to hate her almost as much as she hates me. Although, for the most part, Lindsey just ignores her.

"And your nose is all wrong too." Bristol continues her critique of my artwork.

"Thanks." I pick up the hand mirror we've been sharing to frown at my reflection now. "I broke it in grade school."

"I mean the nose in your drawing, stupid." She laughs.

"Now that you mention it, your real nose could probably use some work too."

I study my nose, which is actually one of my better features. Although it has a little bump in the middle of it, a reminder of the time I fell off the monkey bars. But most of the time I don't even notice it. I check out my lips, too. I suppose I did make them too big in my drawing, but they are naturally full. I look up at where Bristol is still hovering over me and notice that her lips are rather thin in comparison. Not that I plan on mentioning this.

It's ironic because of my new friends—not that I count Bristol as a friend exactly, but out of the girls in our little group—Bristol and I probably look the most alike. We're about the same height, around five foot sevenish, we both have long brown hair, and we're about the same build—averageish. Although Bristol's figure is much better than mine—better than most girls, which she's happy to point out whenever she gets the chance. Another difference is Bristol's eyes are dark brown, whereas mine are a grayish blue.

Still, I wonder if she's extra aggravated over our similarities because of Jayden. I suspect she can't understand why he prefers me to her. From her perspective, she is so much hotter. And for all I know, she might be smarter. She keeps bragging that she has a perfect grade point average. And, of course, she's richer. Not that anyone besides me is aware of my situation. But I think Bristol's dad owns most of Stanfield. So really, in her opinion, she is quite the catch. And if Bristol were just a bit nicer and not so pushy and opinionated, maybe Jayden *would* like her better. In that case, I'm glad Bristol is just the way she is. Except I wish she'd quit looking over my shoulder while I'm working on this ridiculous self-portrait.

"Why aren't you working on your own drawing?" I ask her.

"Because I finished it." She nods to the front of the room. "I already turned it in."

"And you didn't even show it to me." I make a disappointed face, like I want to see it, but mostly I want to get rid of her.

"Oh?" She seems surprised that I'm interested. "Okay . . . I'll go get it."

As soon as Bristol's out of earshot, Lindsey turns to me. "Why do you put up with her like that?"

"Huh?"

"She's being so mean to you. And you just take it. How do you do that?"

I shrug. "Oh, well. Bristol seems to have it out for me."

"Because you're going with Jayden Hammaker."

I try not to look surprised but glance to the front of the room where Bristol is talking, or maybe it's flirting, with Mr. Klein. She's mentioned several times that she thinks he's hot. "Jayden and I are mostly just friends," I say quietly.

"I've seen you with him. It looks like more than just friends to me. And I'm sure Bristol doesn't like it."

I shrug again and return to my drawing.

"I used to be friends with Bristol and Isabella and the others," Lindsey says.

"*Used* to be?"

"I got tired of it." Lindsey lets out a little sigh. "Being *perfect* . . . well, it can be exhausting."

I can't help but smile.

"Here it is." Bristol flits back with her drawing, putting it down right on top of mine.

"Wow, that's really good," I admit. "And it actually looks like you too."

"Well, it's *supposed* to look like me." She smiles smugly. "But thanks."

"You're a good artist," I tell her, feeling Lindsey's gaze on me.

"Maybe . . . but it's nothing I take too seriously." She looks over at Lindsey now. "Not like some people anyway. It's totally unrealistic to think you can make a career as an artist."

Lindsey just focuses back on her own self-portrait. Like everything she does, it's extremely good. She's the most talented artist in this class, probably in the whole school. And I know Bristol's jab was for Lindsey's sake because Lindsey does take her art very seriously. I even heard her talking to Mr. Klein a couple days ago, and she plans to major in art in college. But I don't see why Bristol should pick on her for that. Except that just seems to be who Bristol is — it's like her biggest talent is finding fault with everyone.

"I'm sure a lot of artists would disagree with you," I say to Bristol.

"You mean *starving* artists?" She snickers. "Well, that might be okay for some people, but I happen to enjoy the finer things in life. I suppose my standards are a lot higher than most."

Lindsey looks up from her work, leveling her gaze at Bristol. "Are you talking about *your* standards, Bristol, or your parents'?"

Bristol's dark eyes flash. "Like you'd even know." Then she picks up her self-portrait and saunters back up to the front of the class to chat with Mr. Klein again.

I stare at Lindsey, trying to figure out this puzzling girl. What on earth made her speak out like that to someone like Bristol? Talk about asking for it!

"Yeah, yeah . . ." Lindsey shakes her head like she's disappointed. "I promised myself I wouldn't fight with Bristol this year. Just three weeks in and I blew it."

"Do you usually fight with Bristol?"

She makes a sheepish smile. "Bristol and I have never gotten along too well. But the bickering gets old. I told myself it was time to grow up and move on. But sometimes . . . well, it's like I can't control myself."

I suppress the urge to laugh. "I know what you mean."

"Except that you never stand up to her." Lindsey seems to be studying me now. "Why not?"

I just shrug and return my focus to my drawing and she does the same, and now all I hear is the quiet scritch-scratch of our pencils sketching. I'm sure Lindsey must think I'm totally spineless. And that's fine. Kudos to her that she can take the high road like that—or at least try to. But Lindsey doesn't know what my life is like. She doesn't know the tightrope I'm walking here—between my mom and my new friends. She, and everyone else at this school, is pretty much clueless. And that's exactly how I plan to keep it.

As I join my friends at the lunch table, they're talking about a new movie that just released, making plans to go see it as a group. "You're coming too," Isabella informs me as I sit down with my meager lunch of an apple and soda. My mom was short on cash this morning, and I'm trying to economize however I can, just in case.

"I don't know . . ." I slowly remove my straw from the wrapper, stalling for time since I know a night at the movies isn't cheap.

"Come on," Jayden urges. "It's supposed to be a great flick."

His smile is like a lure. "Okay, I guess I'll go too." But even as I say this, I'm wondering if he's asking me to go with him, like a real date, or whether I still have to figure out a way to come up with the money. Whatever, it looks like I'm in.

"Wow, someone's on a diet," Lily says to me as I take a bite out of my apple.

"Real nice, Adele." Isabella frowns. "Make the rest of us feel guilty for pigging out. You don't even need to lose weight."

"I'm not on a diet. I'm just not hungry, that's all." Okay, that was a big fat lie. Just the smell of Isabella's french fries is making me salivate. Hopefully I won't drool on myself.

After lunch, and as usual, Jayden and I walk to resource together. But to my surprise, he reaches for my hand as we're walking. Naturally, I don't resist. But I am curious, is this just a friendly gesture or something more? Of course I can't ask.

When we're nearly to our resource room, he slows down. "How about if I drive us tonight?" He sounds unsure. "I'll pick you up for the movie around seven. Okay?"

I study him curiously. "Okay . . .?"

He gives me a little sideways grin that makes it seem like he's uneasy. "I mean like a date, Adele."

I laugh nervously. *"Like a date?"* I echo in a teasing tone.

"Unless you don't want to go out with me." Now his cheeks actually flush ever so slightly, and I feel sorry for joking. "I wasn't trying to pressure you into — "

"No, no. I really want to go out with you, Jayden. I was just jerking your chain. Sorry about that."

Now his hazel eyes light up and his grin returns. "All right then!" He squeezes my hand and a rush of excitement surges through me. I am going on a date! *A real live date!*

After school, I meet up with Isabella and immediately tell her the good news, and she seems almost as happy as I am. But

Bristol, who is standing nearby, looks miffed. I'm determined not to let her ruin this for me. And although it's selfish, I suddenly wish that she and Lily hadn't agreed to go to the movies with everyone tonight. For some reason that makes it feel less like a date.

"Who's riding with me?" Isabella asks as she slams her locker closed. "I mean besides Adele." She grins at me as if we have this secret pact because I have been riding to and from school with her for almost two weeks now. And it's so much better than using the transit, not to mention a money saver. Sometimes Bristol rides with us, which puts me in the backseat since, as Bristol pointed out, her house is closer to Isabella's and why should she have to sit in back and then get in front after I'm dropped off. Whatever.

At first I was curious why Bristol doesn't have her own car—especially considering her dad owns the Honda dealership in town. But Isabella confided to me that Bristol got her license revoked last summer. She got into a small wreck while driving with friends in the car (which was breaking the law in our state). Fortunately no one was hurt, but Bristol lost her car and her driving privileges. And since no one is supposed to talk about it, I don't.

"Lily has choir practice, so I guess you're stuck with me, Bella." Bristol gives Isabella her most charming smile. And, as usual, she starts gushing about "old times" and silly events and memories I know nothing about. I think this is Bristol's secret technique for worming her way back into Isabella's inner circle. And for the most part it works. When Bristol wants something, like a ride, she can be extremely charming. And she knows just how to push Isabella's happy buttons. With flattery and jokes she warms Isabella right up, and sometimes they get so chummy

I actually worry that I will be permanently shoved aside. Except Isabella has confessed to me that she doesn't trust Bristol . . . and that I shouldn't either. So it's a weird sort of friendship. And I usually feel caught somewhere in the middle.

"How much longer will you·have to live in Westwood Heights?" Bristol asks me as Isabella turns her car into the condo parking lot.

"I'm not sure," I say as I gather my things.

"It just seems so dismal." Bristol shakes her head. "Your front yard is a giant parking lot."

"But our condo faces the other direction," I point out. "It looks out over the river and it's actually rather — "

"Yes, and our house is by the same river, Adele. Except that our house overlooks the *pretty* part of the river. Not the industrial section."

As I reach for my bag, I can think of no response to that. So much of what Bristol says is like that.

"Tell your mom she better come over and check out the house in our neighborhood," Isabella reminds me. "I heard someone else is interested."

"You mean the Barker house?" Bristol sounds cynical. "That's like a million dollars, Bella. I seriously doubt Adele's mom can afford *that*."

"Unless she's an heiress," Isabella says.

"Yeah, right." Bristol laughs.

"So we'll meet up with you and Jayden at the theater then," Isabella says as I'm getting out of the backseat.

I nod and wave, hurrying through the parking lot toward our condo. I'm thankful to get away, and despite Bristol turning her nose up at Westwood Heights, I still feel extremely fortunate and thankful to be living here. I love unlocking the door and walking into the spacious room with hardwood floors and windows that look out over the river — and I know how to look south to avoid the industrial area. And I don't mind cleaning the granite countertops and polishing the stainless steel appliances. I like keeping it looking good. And I wish we could afford to buy some more furnishings because it's still pretty sparse — not that I plan to bring this up to my mom anytime soon.

But really, this is the nicest place I've ever lived, and my biggest concern is that we could lose it. Of course, I'm trying not to think about that. And right now, the biggest thing occupying my mind is the fact that I am going on my first real date tonight!

'␣ve finally decided on the perfect outfit when my mom enters the condo. It's close to seven now, and I was getting a little worried that she wouldn't get home before I left. I'd tried her cell phone, but it went straight to voice mail. And although there's not much I can do about anything, I am concerned. First my mom acts like we're short on money, and then she doesn't come home at a normal time. It's like a warning, a flag telling me something's not right.

"Why are you so late tonight?" I ask as I come out of my room.

"It's not late." She looks at me like I don't have good sense.

"Well, you obviously went somewhere *after* work." I study her more closely, realizing she's wearing a grubby pair of jeans and a stained hooded sweatshirt. "You didn't go to work looking like that, did you?"

She rolls her eyes, then goes into the kitchen and opens the fridge. As I follow her, that old familiar fear rushes through me. "Did you even go to work today, Mom?" The pitch in my voice gets higher.

"Why isn't there anything to eat in here?" she growls.

"Mom? *Did you go to work today?*"

She turns and scowls at me. "Where are you going tonight? Off to play with your new friends again?"

I'm not fooled by her stall tactic. "You didn't go to work, did you?"

"Who died and made you my mother?"

"Mom . . ." I'm trying to keep my voice calm now. "What's going on? Do you still have your job?"

She laughs, but I can tell by her cynical tone what the answer is. She has blown it. My mom has lost her job. We are going down.

Just then the doorbell rings. "That's Jayden." I hurry to grab my coat and bag. "We're going to the movies. I left a message on your cell." I rush out the door, nearly running Jayden down.

"Whoa, what's your hurry?"

"I'm sorry." I pause and take in a deep breath.

"Are you okay?"

I force a smile. "Sure. I'm fine."

"I was hoping I could meet your mom."

"That's not possible." I struggle to come up with a believable excuse. "That's just the problem. You see, my mom's got the flu, and I was trying to get out quickly so you don't get exposed."

"Oh . . . is she okay?"

"She just needs to rest. She'll appreciate having a quiet evening to herself." And, yes, I'm lying, but what else can I do? As we get into his car, which is not as flashy or new as our other friends' cars but still nice, I dig deeper into my lie. I ramble on about how bad it was when my mom and I both got the swine flu and nearly died and how we take the flu very seriously now.

Finally sick of my lies, I change the subject and make small talk with Jayden as he drives us to the theater. But underneath my nervous chatter, I can't help but be impressed by two things.

First of all, he actually wanted to meet my mom. And second, he seemed to genuinely care about her health. Unfortunately, I don't think he'd understand that my mom's health problems are mental not physical.

We meet up with the others inside the foyer of the theater, where Jayden gets sodas and a big bucket of popcorn — my second meal of the day. All the while I try to keep a cheerful expression and act normal, burying all my fears and worries deep inside . . . wishing I were someone else. Why wasn't I born into a family like one of my new friends? Their biggest worries seem to be whether they'll get into the most elite college, not whether there'll be anything to eat for breakfast tomorrow.

While the movie plays, I'm totally distracted. All I can think about is that I need to figure out an escape plan — for when my mom's ship goes down. Somehow, as impossible as it seems, I have to preserve this nice little life I've been building for myself. Finally, as the credits are rolling, I realize I missed the entire movie. One of my friends will be eager to discuss this intellectual film afterward, and I will be sitting there like a dummy. But I also know what I've got to do to rescue myself and my mom. Tomorrow I will get a part-time job. Somehow I will try to keep our lives from totally unraveling. And then I'll pressure my mom to do her part. She can go beg for her job back, since I know she's lost it. Or she can flip burgers somewhere. I don't really care. But she can't just slip into another deep, dark depression.

"You seem kind of quiet tonight," Jayden says as we go out to his car. "Are you concerned about your mom?"

"I actually am pretty worried." At least that's not a lie.

"Do you want to call to see how she's doing?"

I consider this. "You know . . . I should probably just go

home." The plan was to meet the others at Porky's, this old-fashioned diner that kids from our school hang at sometimes. But my stomach, which should be hungry, feels like there's a chunk of cement sitting in the bottom of it. And I'm not sure how much longer I can keep up this cheerful act. Obviously it's slipping already since Jayden has noticed.

"I understand," he tells me as he starts the car. "And I think it's cool that you care about your mom like that."

"Thanks."

"Hey, should we pick her up some chicken soup or something?"

I force a smile. "That's really sweet, but I think she has what she needs at home. I should probably just be there to help, you know."

After we arrive at my condo, Jayden walks me across the parking lot and up the stairs, holding my hand all the way.

"I'd invite you in, but my mom looked pretty contagious."

"That's okay." He leans toward me . . . and I think I know what's coming. The good-night kiss! I lean forward, holding my breath, and then he gently kisses me on the lips — and I think I see stars!

"I'll call you tomorrow." He releases my hand and abruptly turns, hurrying down the stairs.

With my head still spinning, I stand there in front of my door. I replay the moment, remember the tender kiss — and desperately hope it won't be the last time. Because when I go inside the condo, everything will change. *Bittersweet?* Yes. But I will focus on the sweet for now.

Bracing myself for the conversation to pick up where we left off, I go inside the condo but am surprised the lights are off. I look around and realize that my mom's not home. After I get over being angry, I decide to search for something to eat. I can either have canned soup or macaroni and cheese (from the box). I go for the mac and cheese, and while the pasta is cooking, I run downstairs to the recycling area and pull out a recent paper from the newspaper box, extract the Classifieds, and run back up.

Then as I hungrily shovel in my food, I search through the Help Wanted ads, circling anything with potential. But it's almost like our other town — besides the full-time positions, which are very specific and require degrees, the jobs are for fast-food chains, convenience stores, and, of course, exotic dancers. While pole dancing or whatever they do is among the last jobs on earth I would want, I'm guessing the pay is much more lucrative than clerking at 7-Eleven. Even so, I'm so not going there.

The two jobs that interest me most are for a twenty-four-hour restaurant (the kind my friends would never be caught dead in) and a nursing home. The upside of the restaurant is I could probably eat there. But the nursing home's not far from our condo. And it looks like there are a couple of positions that need filling, which makes me think my mom could work there too. Of course, that's ridiculous on my part to think she'd lower herself to take care of elderly people.

I shove the newspaper aside and take my bowl to the sink, rinsing it and the pan and putting all evidence of my meal in the dishwasher. Where is my mom anyway? It's nearly eleven now and she's still not home. If we were in our old town, I'd assume she was out with friends, but as far as I know, the only friends she has here are work related. And this actually gives me some hope.

"I think Mark Edmonds is crushing on me," my mom confessed to me the first week at her new job.

"Is that why he went to so much trouble to move us here?"

She just gave me a sly little smile. But the message was plain. And to be honest, the idea of my mom getting seriously involved with a successful entrepreneur-type businessman like Mark Edmonds was quite appealing. For that reason and for stability's sake, I encouraged my mom to look her best, to put her best foot forward. And for a while I even entertained thoughts of my mom having someone dependable to take care of her next year, someone to keep her out of trouble after I went away to college. It was a nice little dream. Even when she told me about the little spats she and Mark had been having at work, I had imagined they were just lovers' quarrels or power struggles, rough spots that could be smoothed over in time. Perhaps they still can.

I try my mom's cell phone again, but I'm guessing she forgot to charge it. Even so I leave a message, then hang up. She is with Mark right now. She's probably made up with him, too. And maybe they're discussing the whole work thing . . . making a plan for her to return to her job . . . or maybe he's proposing and they are planning a trip to Vegas. That might upset some daughters, but it would be perfectly fine with me. If I were a praying person, I would beg God to make something like this happen. As it is, I'm not too sure about God. On a good day, I could take or leave him. On a really bad day, I think I don't even believe in God. And why should I since he obviously doesn't believe in me?

Imagining that everything with my mom is getting squared away and I'll have no need for a job, I toss the Classifieds into the trash and go to bed. Really, I was probably just letting my imagination run away with me again. I'm sure that by morning, life will return to normal—well, our recent new-and-improved normal anyway—and all my worries and fears will be a thing of the past.

But morning comes and my mom is still out. I have a can of soup for breakfast and keep myself busy doing homework and laundry. I still can't get over the fact that we have our own laundry room, which is actually a laundry closet—and yet it's so much better than a public laundry facility where you never know what's been in the washing machine before you. I've pulled out some disgusting things.

I wash my mom's sheets, then after they're dried, I remake her bed, all nice and fresh. I imagine that Mom and Mark will come home announcing that they did, indeed, slip off to Vegas last night to tie the knot. Of course, that means we'll have to move, but I know Mark's house is really swanky, and although I'll miss the condo, I'll live closer to my friends' neighborhood.

Finally it's four o'clock and I still haven't heard from my mom. When my phone eventually does ring, it's after five and it's Jayden.

"How's your mom doing?" he asks.

"Uh . . . she's about the same."

"So, you probably don't want to leave her home alone . . .?"

I consider this. "Actually, I don't think she'd really miss me."

"Cool. I thought we could grab a bite to eat and go to the library. I need to find a book for my AP history class before Monday."

"And I've still got homework to do anyway, so I'll just bring it along."

"Great. This will be a study date."

As soon as I hang up, my stomach growls and I can't believe I'm going to have a real meal tonight. I should be more excited about seeing Jayden than eating, but I can't help myself. I'm starving! And although I'm a bit worried that I'll eat like a hog in front of him, I'm not even sure I care. And if I don't hear from my mom by tonight, I think I'll go apply for the restaurant job tomorrow morning. The possibility of having a job that involves both food and tips has suddenly become hugely appealing.

"Wow, you must've been really hungry." Jayden looks at my empty burger basket. I ordered a deluxe double cheeseburger, curly fries, and a chocolate shake (the old-fashioned kind where they bring it in the big metal cup), and I ate every bite.

I smile sheepishly. "I know it's not cool for girls to eat like that—"

"No, I think it's very cool, Adele. I hate it when girls try to eat like an anorexic hummingbird just to impress a guy. Honestly, why is that supposed to be impressive anyway?"

I just shrug, then wipe my mouth with a napkin.

"Seriously, I like a girl who's not afraid to eat."

Now I'm feeling self-conscious. I glance around, then look back at Jayden's basket. He's still got food left. "So, did I really make a pig of myself?"

He chuckles. "No. You have a healthy appetite, that's all. And I like that you're comfortable enough with me to show it."

"Okay . . ." But as we leave I'm wondering if my "healthy appetite" is more off-putting than he's showing. Soon we're in the library, and while he's searching for his book, I settle down to do homework. And I'm surprised that the library is actually quite nice and comfortable, with oversized leather club chairs. The atmosphere in this old building is rather friendly . . . and inviting.

After a while, I need to use the ladies' room, but I'm barely through the restroom door when I'm shocked to find a girl half dressed in there. I try not to stare as I hurry into a stall, then take my time. I'll give her a chance to get her shirt back on. But when I emerge, she's still topless and appears to be using the sink as her makeshift bathtub. I avert my eyes and quickly wash my hands, but when I'm finished, the half-naked girl is blocking the towel dispenser.

"Don't look at me like that," she snaps at me.

"I-I'm not," I stammer as I stand there with my hands dripping. "I just wanted a towel."

"Oh." She glances over her shoulder to see the paper towels, then moves.

I snatch a towel and hurry to dry my hands.

"But I know what you're thinking." She pulls a T-shirt over her head.

I stare at her now. "How can you possibly know what I'm thinking?"

"I know you're judging me, thinking I'm a pathetic loser."

I frown. "Why would I think that?"

She rolls her eyes, then reaches for a backpack that's stuffed to the max. "No reason," she mumbles.

But now I'm curious. "Seriously, why did you think I was like that?"

"Oh, I've seen you and your other rich friends at school, and I know—"

"We go to the same school?"

She frowns. "Not that someone like you would notice. You're too into your own little world to care about anyone else."

I'm about to argue this, but she's actually right. I am too into my own little world to notice. Still, I'm not sure what her point is.

"Anyway, who cares what you think?" She pulls on her jacket, scowling at me like I'm personally responsible for whatever her misfortune is. Or maybe she's just mad at me for finding her half naked in the bathroom.

"I'm sorry you feel that way." I make my way to the door ahead of her.

"Yeah, I'll bet you are."

Then not knowing what more I can say, I just leave and hurry back over to where Jayden is still sitting surrounded by our books and stuff and quickly sit down.

"Something wrong?" He looks curiously at me.

I shrug, then glance over to where the strange girl has emerged from the restroom. "Just a weird encounter in the ladies' room."

"Huh?" His eyes follow mine, then he nods in a knowing way. "Oh, that's Cybil Henderson. She goes to our school. And she's a little odd."

"Oh . . . well, she was half naked in the restroom."

His brows lift. "Seriously?"

I nod. "Pretty weird."

"What was she doing in there?"

"It looked like she was trying to take a bath in the sink."

He frowns now. "I'll bet she's homeless."

"But she goes to our school."

He looks over to where the girl is now standing by the magazines, then shakes his head. "Yeah, well, you know how it is. They'll let anyone in that place." Then he kind of laughs.

I study the girl now. *Cybil Henderson* . . . she goes to our school . . . she bathes in public restrooms . . . maybe she's homeless? And I'm sure I'm just being melodramatic, but *what if that were me?*

t's a little before nine when Jayden drops me off at home. And once again, he walks me to my door and kisses me. And once again, I feel slightly dizzy and warmth rushes through me. Before he can kiss me again, our front door light goes on — making us both jump.

"Looks like your mom's expecting you." Jayden steps back.

"Uh, yeah, I guess I better get inside." I glance behind me to be sure the door's still shut.

"In case she needs something."

"Right." I nod and reach for the doorknob.

"Thanks for going to the library with me," he says as he moves away.

"Thank you."

"I'll call you." And just like that, he's heading down the stairs.

As I go inside, I smell smoke. Not cigarette smoke or cooking smoke, but something different. Kind of like leaves burning. "Hello?" I call out, but no one answers. Is something wrong? Our place is on fire or someone's broken in, so I grab for my cell phone and get ready to dial 911. "Mom?" I call out loudly. "If that's you, you'd better answer — I'm calling the cops!"

My mom's bedroom door opens, and she bursts out with a trail of blue smoke following her. "What are you doing?"

I hold up my cell phone. "I was going to call 911. I thought something was wrong."

She leans her head back and laughs.

"I didn't know I was being funny." I peer behind her. "What's on fire in your room?"

She laughs even harder now. And then a guy appears from behind her. "Whass so funny?" he asks in a slurred voice.

"My daughter. She was going to call the cops on us."

The guy gets a worried look. "Why're you calling the cops on us? We didn't hurt nobody."

"I thought we had burglars." I study him more closely. Although I haven't met Mark, I'm pretty sure this is not him. This guy looks like he needs a haircut and a shave and probably a shower too. "What are you doing anyway?" I look over his shoulder. "And what's burning in there?"

Now he starts laughing. And then they're both laughing like I'm the funniest thing ever. My mom waves her hand at me in a dismissive way. "My daughter" — she lets out a loud chortle — "she thinks she's my mother!"

This makes him laugh even harder. "That's a good one." He pulls my mom back into the bedroom, shutting the door in my face. Then they both laugh some more, and I seriously consider calling the cops. Okay, that would enrage my mom. But who is this guy? And why are they smoking dope in there? Because I know that's what they're doing. And it totally infuriates me.

I go to my room and lock the door behind me. Then I flop down on my bed and try not to remember the last time something like this happened. It's one of those memories you try to suppress, telling yourself it was a one-time-only thing. But history, I've heard, repeats itself. Especially when the person doesn't learn from her mistakes the first time. And my guess is my mom's history is repeating itself now.

I was around twelve the last time something like this happened, about a year after my parents' split. My mom's mood swings had been playing havoc with our lives for months. And then she met Perry, and she started acting almost normal again. At first Perry seemed nice — even to me. He fixed a leaky toilet and promised to take us to Disneyland when he got his tax return. But it wasn't long before I figured out that the connection my mom and Perry shared was illegal drugs. Naturally, my mom claimed she was simply "self-medicating" since her prescription pills never really worked. And naturally, I wanted to believe her. Especially since, as strange as it seemed, our lives had calmed down a bit with Perry around. And then one day I came home from school and my mom and Perry were gone. I mean really gone. A lot of her clothes and things and her leopard-print suitcases were gone.

I freaked. The only other family I knew of was my mom's mom, Grandma Vincent, and she was a person I barely knew and had never wanted to know any better. It's putting it mildly to say that my mom and grandma never got along. Anyway, after my mom didn't come home for three days, I got scared and, out of pure desperation, called my grandma. She was living in Florida at the time and having some health issues related to decades of chain-smoking Camels.

I suppose I actually thought she might come and stay with me so I could finish the school year. Or perhaps she'd invite me to come out to Florida to live with her. I even entertained thoughts about her taking me to DisneyWorld. But my dear sweet grandmother called our state's Department of Children's

Services, and the next thing I knew, I was slammed into a foster home with a bunch of other losers like me.

And if I thought my mom was bad, the foster home was way, way worse. I don't even want to think about it all these years later. But by the time my mom returned and got the authorities to release me back to her care, I'd nearly been raped twice, had a nasty case of head lice, and had developed the beginning of what I'm sure was an honest-to-goodness stomach ulcer.

Now I pace back and forth in my room. I am so angry that I'd like to hit something . . . or throw something . . . or just scream so loudly that all the neighbors come to see what's wrong. I even consider running down to the pay phone and making an anonymous call to the police. But that might land me in the foster-care system again. I am so not going there. To say I'm trapped is an understatement. But what options do I have?

I consider calling Isabella since she's my closest friend. And it's possible I could ask her for help, but she had to go to some out-of-town family thing today. And even if she was home by now, what would I say? Do I invite myself over to spend the night? And if I did spend the night, what if I lost it and just spilled the beans? What would happen if I told her the whole ugly story? I know she wouldn't understand. How could she? Her worst problem in life is a bad-hair day or getting a B on a test. Or the fact that her parents *overprotect* her. She's always complaining about how they keep such close tabs on her. And she can't do anything without checking in every step of the way.

I remember how her mom grilled me when I first met her, like she was worried I might be a bad influence on Isabella. What would her parents think if they knew my mom and some strange man were smoking drugs in our condo right now? For sure, they'd never let me see their precious daughter again.

What would Jayden think if he knew about this? Even as I consider his reaction, I know I will do everything possible to keep him from ever knowing. It would ruin everything between us. I know it. The shame I feel myself . . . just to think about my mom and that creep . . . right here in our condo. It's disgusting. And humiliating. And I hate it. I hate him. I hate my mom. I hate my life.

The next morning, I wake up just as angry as I was when I went to bed last night. I go into the kitchen and start opening and closing cabinets, slamming them so loudly I'm sure our neighbors are ready to complain. Well, let them. And let my mom deal with it!

"What are you doing?" my mom demands when she comes into the kitchen, blinking at me with blurry red eyes. "Are you crazy?"

"Am *I* crazy?" I shoot back at her. "That's novel coming from you."

"What?"

I point my finger at her. "Look at you! You're a big fat mess. I know that you've lost your job. And now you're shacking up with some drug freak and—"

"Watch out what you call my friend."

"Your *friend*?" I let out a big sarcastic laugh. "With friends like that, you don't need any enemies, Mom."

"I'm warning you, Adele; don't you talk to me like that."

"Warning me?" My voice is so loud I'm sure everyone in the complex can hear me. "What are you warning me about, *Mom*? That you've destroyed our lives again? That you blew your last chance to make it? That you're going to start hiding from your problems by using drugs again? Just what are you warning me about? I'd like to know!"

"I'm sick of you and your attitude, Miss Goody Two-shoes! You always talk down to me, like you're so much better. Well, you're not any better, Adele. You've just had more opportunities."

"I've had opportunities?" I shriek at her. "Like working and going to school while you lie around feeling sorry for yourself all the time? Like putting up with a lazy mom who has no idea how to be a mom and is so selfish that it usually feels like she's the child? Like I'm the one who has to be responsible and act like the adult? Opportunities like that?"

My mom is speechless and looks slightly hurt. And I know I should back down. I should apologize and do something to make everything better. The problem is that I'm just fresh out of solutions. And my patience is worn so thin that it's like I'm standing on a paper-thin layer of ice and I don't even care if it breaks and I go down into the freezing waters and drown. I'm so over this.

"That's the thanks I get . . ." She lets out a sob and waves her hand. "For getting us into this place . . . your school . . . your fancy new clothes. That's the thanks I get?"

I place my hands on the granite countertop, bracing myself and keeping myself from picking up something and throwing it. "You might've gotten us here, Mom, but then you blew it up. Just like you always do. You ruin everything."

"You sound like you wish I were dead." She looks at me with steely blue eyes. "Is that what you're saying, Adele?"

Okay, this is the last straw and I know it. I take in a long, deep breath. Be calm. Do not react. Then I look evenly at her. "No, Mom, I don't wish you were dead. I just wish you'd grow up. And if you can't grow up, I just wish you'd go away and leave me alone. Because, seriously, you wear me out. I can't take the drama."

I look down at my hands, and tears slide down my hot cheeks. And I really hate to cry. It feels so weak. I know it was wrong to say all that to my mom, but for the most part, it was the truth. I do feel worn out. I want the drama to end.

So I look up and am about to tell her I'm sorry but that something has to change, and she's not even in the room. I can hear their voices in my mom's room, and I suspect she's telling him about what an ungrateful child I am and how I don't respect her. I don't even care anymore. It's like I'm emotionally drained. The only feeling I'm really cognizant of is that I'm hungry.

I go into my room, get dressed, and put my hair into a tidy ponytail. I put on my coat and get my bag, making sure my old address book is in there because I still have all the phone numbers of the places I worked, and then I head out. I am going to get a job today. My sights are set on the twenty-four-hour restaurant, but since I have to pass by the nursing home, I decide to stop in there as well. River Woods Care Center looks nice enough from the outside. A long, low brick building, neatly kept grounds, lots of windows. It might not be such a bad place to work. Plus it's only a few blocks from Westwood Heights.

"Do you have a résumé?" the middle-aged woman at the reception desk asks me after I explain why I'm here.

"I don't have one, but I can make one if you —"

"No, that's okay." She smiles and bends over to look in a drawer. "Let's see, I know the applications are here somewhere. I don't usually work at this desk, but our regular gal is sick today."

I wait as she pokes around below the desk, then finally pops her head up with an application in hand. "You can fill it out here if you like. There's a dayroom around the corner with tables and chairs."

I thank her and take the application over to what looks like an oversized living room. About half a dozen elderly people are sitting there. Some in wheelchairs, some on the other furnishings, but all sitting separately. As if they don't really know each other. Or maybe they don't want to. There's a big TV going with some kind of sports show on, but no one seems interested. I sit on a molded plastic chair, fish a pen from my bag, and, using my best penmanship, carefully fill out the application.

"What are you doing?" A frail-looking white-haired woman pushes her walker over to the table where I'm writing.

I smile at her. "Filling out a job application."

Her pale blue eyes widen. "To work here?"

I nod. "Do you think I'd like to work here?"

She looks over her shoulder, then back at me with a thoughtful expression. "You seem like a nice girl."

Now I'm not sure what she means by this observation, but I thank her. "Do you think a nice girl would want to work here?"

She lifts a shaky hand to rub her chin. "Well, I suppose a nice girl might want to work here for a while. But not for too long."

"Yes . . . well, it would only be part time."

"How old are you?"

"Seventeen."

She looks shocked. "Oh my. You're only a girl."

"How old are you?"

She gets a sly look. "Twenty-nine."

I try not to laugh.

She lowers her head in a confidential way. "If you reverse the numerals, you can guess my age. I like number games. I used to be a teacher."

I figure she must be ninety-two. And she seems to be mentally sharp, which makes me wonder why she's in here. But I don't think it's polite to ask. I'm sure there are all kinds of reasons elderly people are in here.

"Now I must get my exercise," she tells me as she pushes her walker away. "I fell and broke my hip, and the doctor says the only way I can get better is to walk and walk and walk. And if I get well enough, I can go back to my house."

"Oh, that's good. Yes, be sure you get your exercise."

She pauses. "What's your name?"

"Adele."

"Oh, such a pretty name."

"Thank you. What's your name?"

"I'm Mrs. Ashburn."

"Nice to meet you, Mrs. Ashburn."

Then she smiles and shuffles away. And I turn my attention back to the application. By the time I'm done, I feel rather pleased with myself. For my age, I think my work references are fairly impressive. Hopefully whoever reads this will agree.

"Here you go." I hand my application to the woman at the reception desk.

"That didn't take long." She glances down at the application, then nods. "But it looks like you filled in all the blanks."

"I did my best."

She studies me with interest now. "You know, the manager is on the premises this morning. I'll bet she could see you now if you like."

"For an interview?"

"Why not? Do you want me to buzz her and see if she's interested?"

I agree, and less than five minutes later, I am sitting in front of Ms. Michaels. I'm guessing she's about my mom's age, but she dresses more conservatively and has an air of authority about her. "You seem young to have had quite a bit of work experience." She peers over her reading glasses at me with a curious expression.

I decide to keep everything about this interview as honest as possible. "My parents divorced when I was twelve. My mom has had some health challenges, so I've tried to help out by working when I can. Summer jobs . . . part time after school . . . however I can earn some extra money. The jobs just kind of added up."

She sets down the application. "I can see that."

"And we just moved here in August for my mom's job, but now it looks like she's unable to work. So it's important I find work . . . as soon as possible."

Ms. Michaels nods. "I'm sorry to hear about your mother's poor health. Hopefully she'll get some kind of assistance."

"Yes, that would be good." I'm curious as to what kind of assistance Ms. Michaels is referring to, but I want to stick to the interview. "So, anyway, in the meantime I need to do what I can to help out. And since I live within walking distance, this seemed like a good place to start."

"I noticed you live nearby. And you say you can work evenings and weekends?"

"That's right."

"And I assume these are the correct names and phone numbers for your references?" She studies me closely, as if she thinks I just made them up.

"As far as I know, they're correct." I nod firmly. "I always keep references handy in case I need to find a new job. And I'm pretty sure their recommendations will all be positive."

"You seem like an intelligent girl. And I'm guessing you're a hard worker too. But how are you with elderly people? Do they make you uncomfortable?"

"I've never really known any elderly people, but I don't think I'm uncomfortable with them. I just had a pleasant conversation with Mrs. Ashburn. She seems like a sweet lady."

"She is a dear."

"And she was getting her exercise so she can go home again."

Ms. Michaels frowns. "Yes . . . well, that's not likely. Her daughter hasn't told her yet, but Mrs. Ashburn is a permanent resident."

"Oh . . ." I'm surprised at how disappointed I feel about this. Mrs. Ashburn seemed so hopeful about going home.

Ms. Michaels seems to be observing me very closely, almost as if she's trying to sense my character. "I see you've done some restaurant work, Adele, so I assume you're good at waiting on people, cleaning up messes, getting your hands dirty. Because I'll be up front with you—this isn't a job for princesses. Most girls your age wouldn't be that comfortable helping with the needs of the elderly."

"I'll admit it's not exactly my dream job." And then I confess to her that my next application was going to be for the twenty-four-hour restaurant on Main Street.

"Well . . ." She presses her lips together. "If you're willing, I'm willing. I'd like to try you out here."

"Really?"

She nods and sets my application in the basket on the corner of her desk. "How soon can you start?"

"Anytime you want, I guess." But suddenly I feel a little concerned. What if I'm making a mistake? What if the restaurant job would be a better fit for me? And what about tips? And food?

"How about if you start today?"

I blink. "Today?"

"Is that a problem?"

"I, uh, I just have one question."

"Yes?"

"Well, I don't want it to sound wrong, but one of the reasons I was leaning toward a restaurant job was so I could have some of my meals there." Okay, I'm embarrassed to have just said this.

But she just smiles. "You're welcome to have meals here too, Adele. In fact, some of the seniors would probably get a kick out of it."

"Really?"

"Sure. As long as you work hard and don't spend all your time eating, but I doubt that'll be a problem." She sticks out her hand. "So unless there's a problem with any of these references or your background check with the police, you've got a job." She pauses to look at me. "There won't be, will there?"

I shake her hand. "No, of course not. I've never had any problem with the police."

"I didn't think so."

Okay, my cheeks warm as I recall how close I came to calling the police on my own mother last night. Still, that didn't have as much to do with me as with my mom and her new friend. Not that I plan to mention this.

Now Ms. Michaels asks for my food handlers card, which I give to her. Then she's on the phone talking to someone named Mary. She hangs up and gives me directions to the kitchen. "Mary is our head chef, and she's been needing help in the kitchen. Let's get you started in there and we'll see how that goes."

So, just like that, I am employed. And I will do everything to make sure I stay employed for as long as necessary. I just wish my mom could do the same.

On my very first day of working at River Woods, I put in a whole eight hours. And while I feel really tired as I walk home, I must admit that it really isn't the hardest job I've ever had. The Hot Diggity Dog House was much worse. Even babysitting was harder. The worst part of my day was working with Mary (or Scary Mary as I heard an orderly named Sam call her behind her back). Mary runs her kitchen like she thinks she's an army sergeant. She's probably in her late forties, wears her gray hair in a butch, and is built like a tank. And she had no problem ordering me around and complaining about anything that wasn't done to her specifications.

But at least she seems to know what she's doing. And I was surprised that the food wasn't half bad. Or else I was just too hungry to care. But the potatoes she served were real, not powdered, because I scrubbed them myself. Thankfully, she didn't make me peel them. They were new potatoes with thin skins, and she just cooked them and mashed them with their skins on. She said it was healthier that way. And the roast beef was fall-apart tender and the gravy was actually pretty good too, although I had to pass on the canned peas.

Dinner at River Woods is always served at five o'clock sharp.

That's because the old people go to bed early. The residents are encouraged to eat in the dining room, but some of the ones in really poor health or with special dietary needs are allowed to eat in their rooms. I delivered about a dozen trays and then helped several of the residents eat. That was a challenge, but being cheerful and chatting with them helped a bit. All except for one old woman named Bess managed to eat most of their food. And a nurse named Ellen seemed impressed. That made me feel good. At least it was better than being growled at by Scary Mary.

So as I walk home in the twilight, since it's after seven now, I feel rather pleased with myself. I found a job within walking distance where I get food. And according to my calculations, I made nearly seventy dollars, less withholdings, today. Fortunately my taxes should be minimal, and if my mom doesn't get her act together, I might consider claiming her as my dependent. I don't even feel mad at my mom now. Oh, I'm irritated about her creepy friend, but hopefully my little fit got to him and maybe he's long gone by now.

My plan is to apologize to my mom when I get home. Then I'll do my best to talk her into applying at River Woods too. When Ms. Michaels was giving me my work schedule, I inquired if it would be a problem to have two members of the same family working there, and she assured me that if my mom was willing and able, she would be considered for a job.

Oh, I know that even with both of us working, we won't make nearly as much as she did at her new job. But I figure if she can work full time and if we eat most of our meals at work and really pinch our pennies, we might be able to get by for a while. Besides that, she could let her new car go. I warned her to wait on getting it when we moved here, but she was certain that her old Buick would ruin her image at her new job. Still, without those car payments, plus the saved money on insurance and gas, who knows, we might actually make it.

I'm about a block from home when I check my cell phone, which I've kept off all day (River Woods rules), and am pleased to see that Jayden left me a message. It doesn't say much, except that he was thinking of me and hoped I was having a good day. I actually laugh to consider how shocked he'd be to hear what I'd actually been doing today. Not that I have any intention of telling him, or any of my other friends, about my part-time job. I can only imagine what a hard time Bristol would give me if she knew I spent most of my Sunday with a bunch of old people.

As I cut through the Westwood Heights parking lot, I notice that my mom's little red car is missing from its reserved spot. Disappointed that my mom's not around to hear my recovery plan, I unlock the front door and decide not to let it get to me. Instead, I'll just take a nice long shower and hopefully she'll get home in time for us to talk.

But as I go inside, I get a strange feeling. The lights are turned off, which isn't so unusual. But something just feels different, though I'm not sure what exactly. I turn on the kitchen lights and notice a piece of notebook paper on the island with a strange set of keys on top. I move what appear to be car keys and read the note.

*Adele,*

*Ben and I decided that we all need a break. So he and I are taking a vacation from this place and from you. I'm sorry you think I'm such a disappointment as a mother. Maybe you'll be happier with me gone for a while. These are the keys to Ben's van — the black Dodge parked in the*

*visitor section. He'd appreciate it if you moved his vehicle*
*every other day or so. That way he won't get ticketed by the*
*management.*
    *Take care.*
    *Mom*

I read and reread my mom's somewhat cryptic note, trying
to make sense of it. Where on earth are they going? How long
will they be gone? And how can my mom possibly afford this
so-called vacation? Or is this Ben guy footing the bill? And if so,
where does he get his money since he obviously isn't employed?
And really, what does she even know about him? What if he's
some kind of sociopath serial killer? And where does he get off
expecting me to move his van for him? Think again, Ben! I don't
care if the creep comes home to a truckload of parking tickets.

Still, it's unsettling rambling around our condo knowing
my mom's gone AWOL. I check out her room to see that: (1)
it's a mess—so much for those nice, clean sheets—and (2) she
has packed up most of her stuff like she really plans to be gone
awhile. And I feel a cross between anger and hurt. But there's
another part of me that's not terribly surprised. Kind of like I'd
been waiting for something like this to happen. And yet as I get
into bed, earlier than usual even for a school night, I feel slightly
numb.

The next morning, it's not like I'm doing anything different
than usual as I get ready for school. But for some reason it just
feels different. Maybe it's the being alone part . . . being really
alone. That's different. But I tell myself it doesn't matter as I go
through my usual paces of showering and getting dressed.

Although I know there's nothing to eat in the kitchen except
a couple more cans of soup, I look in the fridge, as if I expect that

yogurt or waffles or orange juice is going to magically appear. Then I finally settle on minestrone soup, which just shows I am hungry because I really don't like minestrone. But it's all that's left. And with a dollar and change in my purse, I wait for Isabella to pick me up. But while I wait, I wonder how long I can keep this up.

It's amazing and slightly weird that none of my friends has any idea of what's going on with me. It's like they just assume that everything in my life is the same old, same old . . . status quo. And really, it's what I want them to think. But at the same time it's a bit bizarre—like I'm leading a secret life. Of course, their oblivion is probably because everyone, including me, is so self-centered and wrapped up in their own lives.

To be fair, I don't really know what's going on with all of them when they're at home with their families. Oh, I assume that their lives are perfectly lovely, that they have delightful parents who really care about them, that there's food in their fridges, and that none of them cried themselves to sleep last night. But I could be wrong.

"How's your mom?" Jayden asks me as we walk to resource together after lunch. "Is she still pretty sick?"

I should be pleased that he cares enough to ask, but just thinking about my mom makes my head hurt. "Oh, she's about the same."

"Well, I told my grandma about your mom getting the flu, and it reminded her that she needs to get her flu shot."

"Does your grandmother live nearby?"

He chuckles. "Yeah, pretty nearby."

"Oh?"

"Didn't I tell you my grandma lives with us?"

"I don't think so . . . not that I recall."

"Yeah. She's got her own apartment in our basement. It's actually a pretty cool setup with a full kitchen and everything. And if I get tired of my mom's cooking, Nana is always ready to whip something up for me."

"Wow, that is a cool setup." I give him a cheesy smile. "I'm envious."

"Well, you'll have to come over and meet her sometime. She doesn't get many visitors."

Now I almost let the cat out of the bag by mentioning Mrs. Ashburn at the nursing home to him. I was about to say how she told me she doesn't get many visitors either, but then I'd have to explain why I was at River Woods. While I suppose I could lie and say I went there to visit, I think the safest plan is to keep the entire thing under wraps. Maybe someday, when I know I can trust Jayden with my secret and when I know he won't dump me for being poor . . . maybe then I can tell him.

After school, Jayden takes me aside. "I need to ask you something before I go to soccer practice."

"What?" Now, for no explainable reason I'm worried. Does he know something about me? Something I don't want him to know?

"I wanted to ask you to go to the homecoming dance with me," he says in an almost shy way.

I nod eagerly. "Sure, I'd love to."

His serious face breaks into a big smile. "Cool."

"That's about two weeks away, right?"

"Yep. The second Friday in October. And if you don't mind, Ethan and Isabella want to go with us."

"That's awesome. Sounds like fun."

He leans down and gives me a quick kiss. "Great. Now I have to get to practice. See ya!"

As he jogs toward the gym, I try to imagine what it'll be like to go to a real dance with my real boyfriend. It feels too good to be true. And naturally, that has me a little worried. But at the same time, I'm too excited to start imagining the worst. Really, don't I deserve to savor this moment? This must be how Cinderella felt when she found out she was going to the ball.

I'm still savoring my invitation to the dance when Isabella seems to appear from out of thin air and Bristol is not too far behind her. "Did he ask you yet?" Isabella asks. "Are you going to homecoming?"

"Yes!" I exclaim. "And he said we're going with you and Ethan."

Isabella lets out a joyful squeal and hugs me. "I can't wait!"

"Looks like someone took her happy pill today," Bristol says in a snarky tone.

"Looks like someone else forgot hers," Isabella shoots back.

Lily comes over to join us. "What's up?"

Isabella quickly relays our "good" news, but Lily (like Bristol) just frowns.

"Can't you at least be happy for us?" Isabella asks.

"Oh yeah, I'm ecstatic." Lily rolls her eyes.

"No one's stopping you from going to the dance," Isabella tells her.

"Right. Except no one asked me." Lily makes a face.

"Why don't you go with Caleb?" I suggest.

Lily's mouth twists to one side like she's actually considering this.

"That's a great idea." Isabella nods.

"Except that someone should include Caleb in on it," Lily says glumly.

"Or you could ask him yourself," Bristol teases. "Nothing quite as attractive as a girl who's desperately begging for a date."

Lily nods. "Yeah, it's a bit pathetic."

"I know," I tell her. "I have Caleb in history. What if I did some gentle hinting?"

"Would you do that for me?" Lily looks hopeful.

"Sure, why not?"

"And if Caleb agrees, we can all go together," Isabella declares.

"And we can hire a stretch Hummer to take us," Lily says with enthusiasm.

"And we'll go to La Bonne for dinner," Isabella adds.

Now Bristol looks seriously aggravated. "It sounds like you'll all have a delightful time." Then she turns to walk away.

"Wait," Lily calls after her. "I thought you were riding with me."

"Oh, if it's not too much trouble," Bristol shoots back. "I'd hate to inconvenience you while you're making all your big plans."

Lily holds up her hand in a phone shape, mouthing "call me" to Isabella, then takes off to catch up with Bristol.

"Poor Bristol." Isabella shakes her head.

"I'm surprised she doesn't find herself a boyfriend," I say as I wait for Isabella to get something from her locker. "I'm sure there are lots of guys who would be glad to go out with her."

Isabella slams her locker shut, then laughs. "Yeah, lots of guys . . . just not the one guy she wants."

"You mean Jayden?"

"Duh." Isabella jingles her car keys. "Hey, we could do some dress shopping on our way home if you want."

"I can't," I say quickly. "My mom's got the flu, and I need to get home to make sure she's okay."

"Well, maybe I'll drop you off and do a little scouting mission myself."

"A scouting mission?"

"For a dress. That way I can pick out the one that's perfect for me, and you and Lily will have to come up with dresses that look good with mine."

"We have to wear matching dresses?" I frown at her. "Like we're bridesmaids?"

"Complementary colors and styles." She looks at me like this should be obvious.

"Oh . . . right." Then I listen as she goes on about all the details and planning that come with the homecoming dance. Who knew there was so much involved? And then it hits me that this is going to cost money. Possibly a lot of money. Money I don't have.

"You're being awfully quiet," she finally says as she's pulling up to Westwood Heights. "Something bugging you?"

"No. Just tired."

"You're not coming down with the flu, are you?" She looks worried. "I hope you're not contagious."

I force a smile. "No, I'm not sick and I'm not contagious." Then I thank her for the ride and tell her to have fun scouting dresses.

"I'll keep you posted."

As she drives away, I realize I need to hurry since my three-hour shift starts at four, giving me about fifteen minutes to get myself changed and to work. Yesterday I wore a nice outfit that ended up getting some food stains on it, so today I want to wear something washable and casual. But this might be a challenge, especially since jeans aren't allowed. And most of my wardrobe is too nice to wear there. Maybe my mom has something I can borrow. We're about the same size, but normally I wouldn't want to be caught dead in most of her clothes. However, I wouldn't want to be caught dead working at the nursing home either. So maybe that's a good combination.

Finally, dressed in a pair of my mom's old cords and a striped blouse that's so last decade, I put on my jacket and desperately hope no one I know sees me as I jog to River Woods for my shift.

"So you came back for more," Mary growls at me as I come into the kitchen. "And you're ten minutes late."

"I punched my time card at exactly four o'clock." I put on an apron. "Ms. Michaels had some paperwork for me to sign." Rule number one if you're working in the kitchen is you must wear an apron and a hairnet — unless your hair is long enough to be securely pulled back in a ponytail, which is how I plan to avoid looking like a cafeteria lady. Not that anyone here cares what I look like, but I still have a tiny bit of pride.

Mary puts me to work chopping onions and then grating cheese with the food processor, which I am slowly coming to terms with. I discovered yesterday that rather than asking her questions (which she hates), it's preferable to dig out an instruction manual (from where they are stored in a big drawer) and just figure things out for myself. I'm thinking it won't be long until I have the big food processor totally down. My goal is to be such a good assistant to Mary that she'll stop griping at me . . . or at least tone it down some. But I suppose I could be dreaming.

Mary hates making small talk in the kitchen, but I can't stop thinking about the dance and how I'll need money, so I take a chance. "Uh, Mary, I forgot to ask Ms. Michaels when payday is."

She lets out a foul word, and I look over to see if she's cut herself. But there doesn't appear to be any blood. "Your second day and you're already whining about getting paid?"

"I just wondered."

"Payday is twice a month. The first and the fifteenth."

I want to ask her if that means I'll get a check in two days since that's the first of October, but I don't want to get yelled at again. Still, I'm hopeful. And unless my math is off, after deductions I should have a check for about a hundred dollars. While it's a relief to think I might have some money, it won't be nearly enough to cover my living expenses, which are meager, as well as what I need for the homecoming dance. Seriously, if I want to go to that dance, I'll need a fairy godmother.

I work quickly and quietly in the kitchen, and I can tell Mary is surprised at how I'm already catching on. Of course, she doesn't say as much, but I spy her glancing my way from time to time. I suspect she's hoping she'll get to scold me for something. But so far I've only given her two opportunities. Once for dropping a knife in the soapy sink water—a big no-no in Mary's kitchen because a person could lose a finger that way. The second scolding was for licking my finger when I wiped a spot of spilled chocolate pudding from the countertop. The irony there is that I've seen Mary lick her fingers numerous times. But I guess when you're the head chef, the rules change.

Mary's shift ends at six, which leaves me to finish the cleanup on my own tonight. But I don't mind. In a way it's kind of peaceful being in the kitchen alone. Also, time passes more quickly when you stay busy. So I'm not complaining. And just like that, my shift is over too. I punch out, grab my jacket, and head for home.

I feel a little uneasy as I walk down the darkened street. But not because I'm worried about muggers or anything. I'm used to being out after dark, and I pity anyone who tries to make trouble for me since I took karate in middle school and I know how to scream at the top of my lungs. In other words, I'm fairly street smart. Mostly I'm uneasy about the fact that my mom is still gone. Oh, I didn't expect her back this soon. And yet I hoped she might call. But I just checked my phone . . . she hasn't.

As I let myself into the condo and lock the door, I feel lonelier than ever. This probably won't last for long. Maybe I should enjoy it a little. My guess is that my mom will be back by the end of the week. Maybe sooner. And hopefully I'll be paid by then and able to stock our kitchen with some food.

I'm just starting in on my homework when my cell phone rings. I grab it up, hoping it's my mom. But it's Isabella.

"I found a dress to die for."

"To die for, huh?" I set down my pencil and listen as she describes what actually sounds like a pretty cool dress. "So, did you get it?"

"Not yet. I thought I should make sure you and Lily approve."

"You need our approval?"

She laughs. "No, of course not. But I wanted you to see it first. I've got it on hold until tomorrow. Can you go with me after school to — ?"

"I can't," I say quickly. Then I go on spinning a lie about how my mom's still really sick and how I need to be here to help her.

"Wow, that sounds serious." Isabella seems genuinely

concerned. "Has she been to the doctor?"

"Not yet. But if she's not better, I might need to take her in tomorrow."

"Well, how about if I send you a photo of the dress."

"Great idea," I tell her. "But really, you should probably just get it. I mean, it sounds gorgeous."

Then she tells me the price and I almost fall over. It would take me a month's salary to buy a dress that costly. Still, I don't act shocked. And when she says it's really a good deal, I agree with enthusiasm. But after I hang up, I realize that I am totally out of my league here. And I will have to think of some way to get out of this dance without hurting Jayden's feelings.

I close my math book, wander out into the living room, and just start pacing. Really, there has to be a way out. Maybe I could tell him I belong to some weird religion where dancing is not acceptable but that I temporarily forgot. Or perhaps I could fake a broken leg. It would be hard to dance with crutches. Of course, that would require money to rent crutches. Money . . . money . . . money. If only there were some simple legal way to get some.

Then I remember something. There have been times when my mom, desperate for money, pawned something of value. And sometimes she'd hold on to the ticket long enough to get the item back after she got flush again. So now I'm strolling around my house looking for items of value. But it's pretty bare bones in here. And I don't really have anything that would bring much. Even my cell phone is a cheapie. And my mom doesn't have any valuable jewelry anymore. Not that I'd consider pawning something like that anyway.

The only things worth considering are the thirty-inch flat-screen TV and Blu-ray DVD player my mom insisted on splurging on. As I recall, they were about four hundred dollars. Still, I can't imagine how angry my mom would be to come home to find that I'd pawned her TV. Of course, it might be what she deserves for abandoning me like this. Finally, I decide that I'll think about that tomorrow. Right now, I have homework to finish.

For the next couple of days, I maintain the charade that I'm still going to the homecoming dance. Not only that, but true to my word, I speak to Caleb on Lily's behalf. And by the end of the day, she too is going to the dance. Now Bristol is the only one not going. But she could go if she wanted to. Obviously not with Jayden, but there are lots of other guys who would ask her, if she'd just give one of them a little encouragement. But it seems she'd rather feel sorry for herself—and aim all her poison darts at me.

At least some of my financial stress is relieved when I actually do get paid. It's not a big check, but I can't believe how comforting it feels to have real money in my purse as well as some food at home. Even so, there's no way I can afford a dress and everything for the dance and still have food to eat. And although I feel guilty, like I'm kind of leading Jayden on, I also keep hoping that something might happen to change my lot. Some miraculous way that would allow me to pull it off. Like maybe my mom would come home with a suitcase full of money. I've imagined Ben and her gambling in Vegas, hitting the big one, and coming home filthy rich. I'm sure I could forgive both of them for everything if that really happened.

I'm also still considering pawning the TV and DVD player. That might bring in enough to get me to the dance. But pretending I'm still going to homecoming with Jayden isn't my only lie. I'm also keeping up the pretense of having a very sick mom at home. So far I've only told Jayden and Isabella these stories. But by midweek, I've already "taken my mom to the doctor," where I was told that it'll be "touch and go" for a while and that "my mom may have to be hospitalized if she doesn't get better."

"So I really need to stick around home," I tell Isabella when she drops me at the condo on Friday, which happens to be my night off—the first day I haven't worked since Sunday. But caring for my mom is the only excuse I can come up with for not going dress shopping with her and Lily this weekend. "You do understand, don't you?"

"Sure, but don't wait too long to get your dress, Adele. All the good ones will be gone."

"I'm looking some online, too," I assure her as I get out of the car. And this is true. I've been searching for bargain dresses and shoes, and to my surprise, there seem to be some real possibilities. The only problem is I don't have a credit card.

I'm just inside the condo, where my mom is still AWOL, when my cell phone rings. It's Jayden. "Hey," I tell him, "I thought you were at a soccer match."

"I am, but it's halftime."

"Who's winning?"

"We are, of course."

"Good for you. I wish I could've come to see it."

"That's okay. I understand. By the way, how is your mom doing?"

"About the same." I turn on the lights in the kitchen. This is pretty much my standard answer now.

"Well, I got an idea. I thought maybe I could come by your

place with a pizza later on tonight."

"But aren't you worried about germs?"

"No, remember I got my flu shot when I took my grandma for hers yesterday."

"Oh, yeah . . ." Now I'm trying to think of some other reason to talk him out of this plan, and yet the idea of spending an evening with Jayden is tempting.

"I just thought I could keep you company. It must get old being stuck at home like that."

I look around the condo and wonder if there's a way I can pull this off. I think I deserve a break after working all week. I imagine Jayden here with me, just the two of us. And pizza, after a week of old folks' dinners, sounds heavenly. "Okay, come on over."

"Great! So I'll see you around seven."

"Can't wait." As I hang up, I wonder if I've made a mistake. I could be blowing my own cover. But already I'm concocting a plan. "Mom" will be barricaded in her room—I'll even make it look like someone's in her bed just in case. But she'll be resting, and other than bringing her a cup of tea at some point in the evening, she will not want to be disturbed.

As a result, Jayden and I will have the rest of the condo to ourselves. That's when I notice the place has gotten a little messy. I've kind of let things go, thanks to my job at River Woods. So I do some quick cleaning, and in an attempt to make the living room look more furnished than it really is, I do some quick rearranging. I rob both my room and my mom's for a few more furnishings—a couple of lamps, some pillows, and a throw—which all help to make the place look less stark.

Then I run down to the market and get some sodas to stock in the fridge. This will stretch my frugal budget a bit, but it'll be worth it. I want Jayden to think I live a somewhat normal life. And I can explain that my mom was too busy with her job and then the sickness to get our condo tricked out just how we wanted it. I think he'll understand. I can also tell him that we decided to wait to get real furniture until we get into a bigger house — in order to get things that fit it better. My make-believe life sounds almost believable to me.

It's about six thirty when the doorbell rings, and thinking Jayden's here early, I happily open the door. But to my surprise it's a man in an expensive-looking suit.

"Is Carlene here?"

I blink and try to figure out who this guy is. The expression on his face is serious. Is he an attorney? A well-dressed cop? Someone from Children's Services perhaps?

"I'm sorry." He reaches into a pocket and pulls out a business card. "I'm Mark Edmonds. I was Carlene's boss."

"Oh right. I'm her daughter, Adele."

Now he blinks in surprise. "Carlene has a daughter?"

I just nod.

"Oh . . .?" He looks stumped.

"Anyway, she's gone right now."

"Well, I've been trying to reach her on her phone, but she must not be checking her voice mail."

I shrug. "I guess not."

"When do you expect her back?"

"I . . . uh . . . I'm not sure." Now I feel hopeful. Is Mark here to offer Mom her job back? To say he's sorry? Maybe he wants to marry her.

"Because I really need to talk to her. It's urgent."

"Maybe if you tell me, I can get a message to her."

He seems uncertain. "Yes, I suppose that's a good idea.

Here's the deal: I gave your mom an advance on her salary." He shakes his head like he can't believe what a fool he's been. "And I paid her rent for the first two months in the condo. But when your mom walked out on her job, I told her I expected to be recompensed for all the expenses. After all, we had an agreement and I trusted her, but she let me down."

That old feeling, like there's a brick in the pit of my stomach, returns as I stand there wishing I could say something to smooth this over. I even consider telling him that my mom has a really bad case of the flu, that she'll return to her job as soon as she gets well, but I have a feeling he won't buy that.

"So, anyway, the property manager called to tell me the rent was overdue on your condo. Naturally, I have no intention of paying it."

"Naturally."

"So unless your mom pays her rent, it looks like you'll be evicted."

"Evicted?"

He nods glumly. "I'm sorry. It doesn't seem fair to dump all this on you. But you look like you're old enough to handle the truth. Tell your mom that if she doesn't make some kind of an arrangement to pay me — rather the company — back, we'll be forced to hire an attorney."

"Right . . ."

"You'll let her know I came by then? Tell her that she needs to take responsibility for these things before it's too late?"

I just nod, knowing full well it's already too late.

"Thank you." He forces a smile. "Hopefully you'll learn from your mom's mistakes and never end up in a situation like this yourself."

"Hopefully." I match his forced smile with one of my own,

then he tips his head and leaves. I close and lock the door, replaying his warning. *"Never end up in a situation like this myself . . ."* Is this guy nuts? I'm already in a situation like this! It's my mom who ran away. And now I'm being evicted? What am I supposed to do?

## CHAPTER 8

"Maybe this wasn't such a good idea after all," Jayden says as he lays down the last of his cards, going out and winning his second game of rummy.

"Playing cards?" I toss my cards aside and frown at him. "After all, you're winning."

"No, I mean coming over here while your mom is so sick. I can tell you're pretty worried about her."

"Oh . . ." I nod. "I guess I have been a little distracted."

"Do you need to check on her or anything?"

I stand and look at my watch. "Yes, it's time for her medicine. And I should probably take her something to drink."

"And I should probably go." He stands, then pulls me into a hug. "Tell your mom I'm sorry I didn't get to meet her."

"I will."

He leans down to kiss me, and suddenly I want to hang on to him and I wish he wasn't leaving. And I'm mad at myself for not making this evening more fun. What if Jayden decides I'm boring or not worth it or just gets tired of hearing about my sick mom all the time? Or even worse, what if he figures out I've been lying to him? Why didn't I just tell him the truth in the beginning? Maybe he would've understood. Now it feels too late.

"I'll call you," he says as he leaves. I lock the door and lean my head against it. My life feels like it's unraveling . . . and fast. What am I going to do? *What?*

I cannot ignore Mark Edmonds' warning about getting evicted. I remember the time Mom and I got evicted a few years ago. I came home from school to find an eviction notice taped to the front door and all the locks had been changed. Everything we owned, which wasn't much, was still inside, but we weren't even allowed to get it. We spent the night at my mom's boyfriend's house. I can't even remember his name now, but he called the landlord and talked him into letting us have our stuff back. The next morning we went over to our house to find all our belongings strewn across the front yard. I remember feeling so humiliated as I gathered up my things with neighbors watching. One lady even stopped by to ask if we were having a garage sale.

Think . . . think . . . I pace back and forth in the living room. Then I notice the van keys on the counter and remember I haven't moved Ben's van since Wednesday night. I almost didn't move it at all except I didn't want to give that creep any excuse to park himself at our condo when (or maybe if) he and my mom came home. But now I'm thinking that van might be my only hope of holding on to my stuff, because if I come home from work tomorrow to find this place locked up . . . well, I'm not sure what I'd do. Probably end up in a foster home wearing somebody's hand-me-downs to school next week.

I pocket Ben's keys and head straight for my room, gathering up clothes and shoes and packing them in my duffel bag. I realize it's going to take a few trips. I also remember how smelly that van was, and I can only imagine what kind of junk might be in the back of it. So leaving my duffel bag in the house, I arm myself with cleaning products and garbage bags and go down to work over that van. I bag up a bunch of what I assume are Ben's clothes and personal items and drag these back upstairs, dumping them in my mom's room. Let her deal with them.

Next I park the van by a dumpster and throw the rest of the junk away. Then I move the van, which I have named Darth Vader, over on the side of the street beneath a streetlight. And now I sweep and scrub and eventually decide old Darth Vader might not be so hopeless after all. It's after eleven by the time I park Darth in my mom's parking space close to our unit. Although I'm exhausted, I spend the next hour hauling everything I want to keep down to the van. I even put the TV and some other items that might be worth money down there. All my efforts might be futile if my mom and Ben show up, but it's a chance I'm willing to take. For all I know, I could be living in that van before long.

With that in mind, I go back upstairs and launder my mom's bedding, which I plan to confiscate and carry to the van just in case. I'll remain in the condo for as long as I can, sleeping in my own bed. But if I get locked out, I'll have everything I need in the van. It seems crazy to go to these extremes. And I know I'll have some explaining to do if my mom shows up tomorrow. But she'll have some explaining to do as well!

Finally, I fall into bed exhausted. Thankfully, I don't have to go to work until eleven so, unless I'm evicted first thing in the morning, I will sleep in.

The next morning, I take a few more things down to the van. If I end up having to live in it for a while, it'll be like camping. It might even be fun in a twisted sort of way. Then I walk around the condo, looking at it long and hard, knowing full well this might be the last time I see it, and I drive the van to work.

My job, I've decided, is a great distraction. The work keeps me so busy I don't even have time to think or obsess. And when I do have a free moment, I usually end up visiting with one of the residents. When my shift is over, I actually start to walk home before I remember Darth Vader back in the employee parking lot.

Tonight I park the van in the visitor lot. I think it's probably better if the manager doesn't figure out that the van has any connection to our condo. I get my old backpack, which I've stuffed with everything I need for the night, then glance around to see if anyone is watching me before I quietly sneak up the stairs, fully expecting to see an eviction notice on the door. But there is no letter and my key works in the lock. So I get to sleep in my own bed again.

On Sunday morning, I can almost make myself believe that my fear of being kicked out of this place is all in my head. Even so, I don't leave anything I want behind. And after another busy day at work, I come home and sneak up the stairs with my backpack only to find there actually is an eviction letter posted on the door. And a lockbox prevents me from using my key. I scan the letter, and my mom has been instructed to contact management immediately. Like that's going to happen.

But just in case, I will leave one more message on her cell phone. I've already left a bunch, even informing her of Mark's visit and the warning about the eviction. But when I turn on my phone, I discover that it's out of service, which I'm guessing means that my mom hasn't paid that bill either.

I'm tempted to just chuck my phone as far as I can throw it, but that's not too prudent. Instead I return to the van and have a good long cry. This is so wrong. Life is so unfair. I work so hard . . . I try to make the best of a really messed-up situation, and I end up living in an old van. Wrong, wrong, wrong.

Now I realize that I haven't even done my homework. But to do it in the van means I'll have to use a light to see, and I know that could run down the battery. I consider driving somewhere, like a coffee shop, where I can sit and study, but there's only a quarter of a tank of gas. I can't afford to waste a drop. Think . . . think . . .

I remember the library isn't too far away, and I decide to go there to do my homework. I just hope I don't see anyone I know because I'm still wearing a work outfit (my mom's old clothes) and I'm badly in need of a shower. I grab my backpack, and as I'm going into the library, I remember the girl in the bathroom — the homeless girl.

That girl is now me.

In the library, I go straight to the bathroom where, feeling the full humiliation of being homeless, I clean up as best I can in a sink. Then I use a stall to change my clothes. I only do this because I'm worried I might run into someone I know, and I can't bear the idea of being seen in my work outfit. Then I brush out my hair and find a table in a corner where I start doing homework. The library closes at nine so I have just a little more than an hour to finish up.

"Hey, Adele." I nervously look up to see Lindsey Nelson from my art class, wheeling a book cart toward me. "What are you doing here?" she asks in a friendly tone.

"Homework." I force a small smile. "That's a lot of books. Are you checking them all out?"

She chuckles. "No, I'm a student aide here."

"A student aide?"

"Yeah, I volunteer."

"That's nice of you."

She shrugs. "It's not as nice as it seems. My mom's the head librarian, and she promised me a trip to Europe after graduation if I put in a whole year as a student aide."

"That's cool." I nod like it's just a normal thing—a mom who gives her daughter a European vacation like that . . . big deal. But inwardly I'm seething with envy. Why didn't I get a mom like that?

"So I'll let you get back to your homework." She picks up a book from her cart, checking its spine. "I need to reshelve these."

"Later." I turn my focus back to calculus, but all I can think about is how unfair life is. Totally and irrevocably unfair.

Despite a restless night, I wake up early. Sleeping in a van will take some getting used to. My plan is to drive to school, where I will slip into the locker room, grab a quick shower, and get dressed and put together in time for my first class. My biggest concern will be running into someone I know, although that seems unlikely since none of my girlfriends frequent the girls' locker room. But just in case, I've already fabricated a story. I'll just say the water was turned off in our condo or something to that effect. I have a feeling it's not as much *what* I say, but *how* I say it that matters. I must manufacture confidence.

Fortunately I don't see anyone I know and I have safely deposited my bulging backpack into my locker just as Isabella calls out my name.

"Where have you been, Adele? I've been worried sick about you."

"What do you mean?"

"I called and called, and your phone's not working. I stopped to pick you up for school this morning, and you weren't in the parking lot." She has a stricken look. "Is it your mom? Did she get worse? Is she in the hospital or something?"

Okay, I know this is crazy, but I just go with it. Nodding and trying to look seriously worried, I tell Isabella that my mom really has gotten worse. "It's turned into pneumonia."

Her hand flies to her mouth. "Oh no."

"Yes. Very serious."

"I'm so sorry. Is there anything I can do?"

I shake my head. "No, it's just that I have to spend a lot of time with her, and I'm a little stressed. And I guess she forgot to pay the cell phone bill, you know, because she's been so sick." I sigh. "Life is a mess."

Isabella hugs me. "I'm so sorry, Adele. That's just horrible. Well, if there's anything I can do, just tell me. You know I'm here for you."

"Thanks." I release a shaky-looking smile.

She pats me on the back. "That's what friends are for."

"I really appreciate it. I guess I should get to class."

As we part ways, I'm thinking this "mom in the hospital" story could really work for me. It will explain why no one is home, why I'm a little rattled, or why I might do something like grab a shower at school. Naturally, after spending the night by my nearly dead mother's side, I don't have time to run home and do it. Okay, I know it's lame, but I think maybe I can pull it off. What choice do I have?

By lunchtime, all of my friends have heard the "news" that my mom is "at death's door." And everyone is extremely kind and surprisingly thoughtful. Even Bristol is being unusually nice. It's hard not to like this.

"Do you need a ride over to visit your mom?" Isabella asks.

"No, I'm using her car now," I lie.

"Oh right." She nods. "How about your phone? How do you call her?"

"She's in bad shape, so she can't really answer the phone," I lie some more. "But I just used the pay phone to check with the hospital."

"And how was she?" Jayden asks with concern.

"The same." I sigh for drama.

"What about the homecoming dance?" Isabella asks. "Please tell us this doesn't mean you can't go."

I look sadly at Jayden. "I'm not sure."

"Hey, no problem," he tells me.

"I really want to go, but it's hard to say."

"Don't worry," he assures me, "we'll just play it by ear . . . see how it goes. I understand, Adele."

"I appreciate that."

"But if your mom gets better?" Isabella looks hopeful. "You'll go to the dance then, right?"

"Of course."

"But what about your dress?" Isabella's brow creases. "I'm guessing you couldn't get one with everything that's going on with your mom."

"No, I just haven't had time." I frown and wonder just how deep I'll have to get into this . . . before I get buried alive.

"Don't be pestering Adele about dresses," Jayden tells Isabella. "I'm sure that's the least of her worries right now."

"That's true," I tell him. And I am so not lying about this. Yet this attention and concern from my friends feels strangely good. Like I could get used to this. I even toy with the idea of letting my mom "die" in the hospital. Okay, that's pretty extreme. Even for me. But it's tempting.

By the end of the day, I come up with an even better plan.

I will have my mother get a little better in the hospital, but she'll be too ill to come home. So by the end of the week, I'll have her sent to a nursing-care facility to recuperate. There she will lie low until I can figure out some other kind of long-term answer . . . or until she comes home. That is, if she's coming home. And more and more, I suspect she's not.

In the meantime, I'll see how much money I can get for some of the stuff in the van. Not only will it make more room, but it might finance a way for me to go to the homecoming dance. Because I am going. I deserve to go! And I just need to accept there is no such thing as a fairy godmother. No one is going to come to my rescue—nobody besides me. This Cinderella will create her own magic.

After school I'm about to rush off—partly to make a get-away in Darth Vader without being observed and partly because I have "business" to take care of—when Isabella stops me.

"What's your hurry?"

"I need to get to the hospital and check on Mom."

"Which hospital is it?" Lily asks.

"Yeah," Isabella says, "we want to send her some flowers."

"Uh . . . I can't remember the name offhand." I pause, trying to think of an answer. "I mean, everything happened so fast with my mom, and I'm still trying to figure out this town and—"

"Well, it's either Saint Andrews or—"

"Oh, yeah." I suddenly remember something I saw in the nursing home. "I totally forgot. My mom can't even have flow-ers. It has to do with the pollen or germs or something. But there's a sign on her door that says No Flowers. Thanks anyway, and I'll tell her you guys were thinking of her." I glance at my watch. "I really need to run now."

They're still standing around talking as I hurry away. I want to get to Darth Vader without having to explain why I'm driving this big, ugly van instead of my mom's car. Although I'm already working on a story to explain that one, too. My life, like a house of cards, seems to be fabricated of flimsy lies these days. I just hope no big wind comes along to blow it all down. Or that I don't get my stories mixed up. I'm actually thinking about writing down all my lies in the back of my notebook just to help me keep track of them.

On my way to work, I swing by the pawn shop I noticed when I was driving to the library last night. I park in back, then go inside to see a short bald man hunched over behind the counter; he's reading a gun magazine.

"Excuse me, I — uh — I've never done this before so I'm not really sure of the protocol."

He looks up over his reading glasses and chuckles. *"Protocol?"*

"I have some items I need to sell. Do I just bring them in here or what?"

He frowns. "What kind of items?"

So I tell him about the TV, DVD player, and some of the other things. "They're all pretty new."

"Why are you selling them?" He peers curiously at me, almost like he's suspicious. "You know we have cops coming in here regularly. So if they're stolen goods, you'll be — "

"No, no," I say quickly. "I swear to you they're not stolen." And then I decide to tell him the truth. Or mostly. I explain how my mom ran out on me and how the rent was overdue. "And I got evicted. So I'm working part time at River Woods Care Center, and I'm trying to scrape up enough money to find another place to live . . . so I can stay in school." Then just in case he's concerned about my age, I add, "It's my first year in community college, and I really don't want to lose my credits."

He nods. "Yeah, that's tough. My parents weren't much good either." He folds his newspaper closed. "Well, go ahead and bring it on in here. If it's as new as you say, I'm sure I'll be interested."

So I make several trips, carrying in the TV, small kitchen appliances, lamps, and everything. Even though he doesn't give me close to what I know my mom paid for all that junk, I do end up $360 richer. "Thank you," I tell him.

"And you stay in school," he says with a wink.

I nod eagerly. "Don't worry, I plan to. Now I better hurry if I want to make it to work on time. Thanks again!".

As I drive to work, I'm surprised at how good it felt just then to tell the truth. Or mostly the truth. This house of lies I'm building is a scary thing . . . and I'm sure in time it will cave in on me.

G enevieve, a nurse's aide at River Woods, is the only person there even close to my age. As a result, she and I some-times take our break together. She's fun and laid back and good for a few laughs. Plus she's really good with old people. I know she has an apartment not far from work, and I had even hoped I might rent a room from her. But during our evening break, she confides that her boyfriend is moving in with her this week.

"Naturally, I can't tell my mom about it." She makes a face. "She is so freaking conservative; she'd have a total fit."

"She sounds like the opposite of my mom," I confess.

Genevieve gets a sad look. She is one of the few people on the planet who knows about my situation. Not everything, of course, but she knows about my loser mom. "Still haven't heard from her?"

I shake my head. Then to change the subject, I tell her about the upcoming dance. "I really want to go, but it's going to be so expensive. I'm thinking I should just forget it."

"Why does it have to be expensive? Doesn't the guy pay for most of it? Or has that all changed since I was in school?"

"Oh, you know, dress . . . shoes . . . it all takes money." I haven't told Genevieve about the eviction or how I'm "camping" in a van. I'm not sure if it's because I don't totally trust her or if it's my pride.

"Hey, I have some old formals." She studies me. "I'm guessing we're about the same size. Want to borrow one?"

I consider this. An "old" formal sounds a bit dismal. I imagine pink puffs and ruffles and am about to say "thanks but no thanks."

"Yeah, yeah . . ." She rolls her eyes. "I know what you're thinking. That they'll be like ugly bridesmaid dresses. But I swear they're not bad. One of them is actually kind of elegant in a little-black-dress sort of way." She holds her index fingers and thumbs like she's framing me. "In fact, you'd probably look very classy in it. Put your hair up, some fake diamonds. Very Audrey Hepburn."

Okay, now my interest is piqued. "Really?"

She nods. "Yeah. It's a very sweet dress. Great lines, sequins, really sweet. It's so cool that I've actually worn it a few times. I might even wear it again if Adam ever looks like he's getting ready to pop the question. Or maybe for New Year's."

"Are you sure you want to loan it out?"

"Why not? You seem like a very nice person, Adele. I'm sure you'll return it to me in the same condition that—"

"I could get it dry-cleaned afterward."

She waves her hand. "Oh, that probably won't be necessary."

"But I need to check with Isabella first."

"You're going to the dance with a chick?"

I laugh. "No. But Isabella is my friend, and she wants our dresses to go together."

"So call her."

Now I explain about my cell phone and she hands me hers, but then I realize I'll probably have to lie about my mom in front of Genevieve. So I quickly explain about my rich friends

and how they wouldn't understand about my runaway mom.
"So I've kind of made some stuff up about her being sick."

Genevieve just shrugs. "Hey, I don't blame you a bit." And
so with her listening in, I call Isabella.

"Who's Genevieve?" Isabella asks me after I say hello. She
must've seen the name on her caller ID.

"She's a nurse at the hospital," I say, which isn't a complete
lie. "She let me borrow her phone."

"Oh good. So, how's your mom doing?"

"She's a little better. And it sounds like if she improves,
they'll move her to a nursing-care facility until she gets strong
enough to go home."

"That's great news."

"Anyway, Mom thinks I should go to the dance and—"

Isabella lets out a happy yelp.

"And I found this dress online that's really cool. Kind of a
little black dress with sequins—very Audrey Hepburn."

"Ooh, that sounds perfect."

"Okay. I guess I'll order it then."

"Better have them ship it next day. Just in case."

"Yes, I'll do that."

"Oh, I'm so glad you get to go. Give your mom a kiss for
me!"

"I will." We say good-bye and I hand the phone back to
Genevieve, then blow a kiss in the air.

"What's that?"

"A kiss from Isabella for my mom."

Genevieve laughs. "You are going to look totally hot in my
dress. Make sure you get some photos at the dance."

I reach out and hug her. "Thank you! You're like my fairy
godmother."

She hugs me back. "I'd offer to loan you some shoes, but I really don't have any that look good enough to go with that dress right now. Plus, I doubt we're the same size. I have really big feet."

"I'll splurge on new shoes."

"Cool."

And then it's time to go back to work. But thinking about that Audrey Hepburn dress has me so happy that I temporarily forget my life is such a mess. It's not until I punch my time card and realize I'm going home—"home" to Darth Vader—that the old heaviness returns. And honestly, if River Woods had an empty bed, I would consider climbing in and pretending to be a resident. I've actually considered grabbing a shower here, but I'm afraid I'd get caught and have to explain myself. And what if I lost my job? That's a risk I can't afford.

Worried I could run into Lindsey at the library, I go to a coffee shop to study tonight. But first I put twenty bucks' worth of fuel into Darth Vader. Next I go to the cell phone store at the strip mall and make a payment, which gets my phone service back. It's not so much that I need a cell phone myself, although my friends are a little worried; mostly I'm getting concerned about my mom. What if she's trying to get ahold of me? And as unrealistic as it seems, I keep expecting her to call and tell me what's up. Like I think she's going to show up and magically put our messed-up lives back together.

I finish my math, but despite two cups of bad coffee, since I can't go into Starbucks for fear of seeing someone I know, I'm so tired I can barely keep my eyes open to read *The Grapes of Wrath*. If I still had a TV and DVD player (or a home), I'd be tempted to just watch the movie. Although I used to consider that sort of thing cheating. Why should it matter now when in so many other ways I feel like a cheat . . . and a liar . . . and a phony?

Tuesday and Wednesday pass . . . slowly. And with no word from my mom, I go to work and to Darth Vader and to school . . . and then do it all over again. The only "upside" is I'm so exhausted that I'm finally able to sleep in the van reasonably well. And lately I've been parking Darth at the visitor lot at the condo or the employee lot at River Woods. So far, no one seems to notice or care.

The wind-up alarm clock, which I got at Wal-Mart along with a few other necessities, goes off at six thirty in the morning. I climb into the driver's seat, blurrily drive across town, then hit the showers in the girls' locker room by seven. I dress as neatly as I can, which is getting more challenging, then go to my classes, where I'm trying to keep up.

I hang with my friends I'm trying to keep fooled. Then I go to the nursing home, where I don't have to fool anyone. Finally when my shift ends, I head for the library, where I use their bathroom to clean up and change clothes, then study until closing, sometimes napping in the big leather club chairs. I don't even care if I see Lindsey there.

By Thursday morning I feel exhausted. So tired I don't know how I can go on . . . or if I even want to. My game of charades isn't helping either. It's hard to keep track of your lies when you're totally worn out.

"Are you feeling okay?" Lindsey asks me in art. "You look like you're sick or something."

I sit up straighter. "I'm just tired."

"That's because she's practically living at the hospital," Bristol shoots back at Lindsey in my defense. "Her mom's seriously ill, you know."

It's weird having Bristol stand up for me like this. But for some reason, this lie about my mom has really softened her heart. So much so that I almost wish it were true. Not that I want my mom to suffer like that . . . well, not too much anyway. But having Bristol's sympathy is kind of nice.

"I thought it was because you stayed too long at the library last night," Lindsey says to me. "I saw you leaving right before closing."

"You were at the library last night?" Bristol questions me.

I shrug. "I needed a book for AP history, and then I decided to stay there and study. It's kind of lonely at home. You know, with my mom gone."

Bristol nods. "Yeah, that must be hard."

"What's going on with your mom?" Lindsey asks.

So I repeat the story I've been telling the rest of my friends. But Lindsey has this questioning look, like she's not really buying it. So I change the subject. "Lindsey, which countries will you visit in Europe next summer?"

Fortunately Bristol gets interested in the Europe trip too. And for the first time this year, the three of us are acting almost like we're friends. Even Mr. Klein seems to notice.

"Nice to see everyone getting along today." He pauses to examine our charcoal sketches.

And it is nice. I feel somewhat encouraged. Like maybe I can keep this act up for a while longer. Plus there's the dance tomorrow — that's something to look forward to. My big night . . . where I get to do my Cinderella act and pretend I'm a real princess.

I haven't even had a chance to get my shoes or any accessories yet. But this afternoon I'm going to run over to a place Genevieve told me about — a shoe store not far from work that's supposed to have a fantastic selection of designer knockoffs at some very affordable prices.

"I have to hurry," I explain to Isabella after school. "Mom's getting moved to the nursing-care center this afternoon."

"Oh, that's so good to hear." She smiles. "Let us know if she can have flowers there."

"I will." Even as I say this, I consider telling her that my mom has been moved to River Woods, but I'm not sure I want that much information floating around. I don't want to jeopardize my job. So I just grab my bag, wave to my friends, and dash off. Their sympathetic glances are touching. And despite how pathetic my life really is, I almost feel lucky.

I feel even luckier as I'm shoe shopping. "These are a perfect knockoff of Louboutins," a stylish salesgirl tells me as I'm trying on a pair of strappy black sandals. "And we only have them in a size eight, which looks absolutely perfect for you."

"Louboutin?" I try walking in the high heels.

She gives me a slightly disparaging look. *"Christian Louboutin,"* she says like I should know this name.

"But why is the sole red?"

She laughs, then just shakes her head like I'm hopeless.

"They are pretty," I admit as I continue to practice walking. I'm not used to such high heels.

"They are gorgeous. If they were my size, they'd be gone."

"Oh wow," a young woman says to me as she checks out my feet. "Christian Louboutin, right?"

I kind of shrug. "I guess."

"Do you have any more?" the woman asks the salesgirl.

"Those are the only ones — size eight."

The woman frowns at me. "Are you getting them?"

I glance at my watch, then nod. "I think so."

Before long, the shoes are bagged and I run into an accessories store right next door. There, following Genevieve's advice, I get some faux diamond earrings and a necklace. I make sure the pieces aren't so flashy as to look fake. And then I hurry to work.

During my break, I show Genevieve my purchases and she is very impressed. "Do you have the dress with you too?"

"It's in my car."

"Go get it," she commands. "Let's do a dress rehearsal and see how it looks."

I dash out to the van, where the dress is hanging in the plastic bag I put over it to protect it. I hurry back into the restroom, where Genevieve is waiting for me, and before long, she helps me get completely dressed.

"You look so hot," she says as I stand in front of the mirror. "I think the dress looks even better on you than me." She lifts up my hair. "You need to give it a little twist like this and pin it up. Then let a few tendrils down. See what I mean?"

I nod, taking this all in. "Thanks so much. There's no way I could've pulled this off without you."

She grins. "Just make sure you have a great time."

Seeing that our break's almost over, I quickly but carefully remove my glitzy outfit and put my work clothes back on. Then as I hurry to return my things to Darth Vader, I wonder how easy it will be to get dressed and looking good inside of the cluttered van tomorrow night. Maybe I'll have to come up with a better solution for a dressing room.

"You seem happier than usual tonight," Mrs. Ashburn says to me as I'm helping her get ready for bed. She's my favorite resident, and I'm always eager to assist her in any way I can. This actually works out fairly well, since some of the nurses say she talks too much. But I don't mind her chatter.

I tell her about tomorrow night's dance, and she launches into a story about her first dance back when she was in high school. "It was the graduation ball," she tells me with a faraway look. "And I thought Lawrence Barnes was the cat's pajamas." She chuckles. "You girls don't use that expression these days. But Lawrence was truly dreamy. He looked just like Dick Powell."

I nod as I help her sit on the edge of her bed.

"I was simply over the moon when he asked me."

"So, he wasn't your boyfriend?"

"Goodness, no." She giggles as I fluff her pillow and help her lean back into it.

"What did you wear?" I pull the bedspread and fold it neatly down, just how she likes it.

"I can remember the dress as if it were yesterday . . ." She closes her eyes. "Butter yellow taffeta trimmed with chocolate brown velvet ribbon. Sweet little puffed sleeves. And the bodice fit me like a glove." She sighs. "I had a good figure back then. And the skirt was so full. It spun out in a circle when I danced."

"It sounds beautiful." I notice she hasn't taken her nighttime meds yet so I hand her a plastic cup of water and the small paper cup with the pills.

"Oh, it was. I'm sure I have photos somewhere . . . in my home."

I know Mrs. Ashburn well enough to know this is a dangerous subject. Her home, where she wants to return as soon as she is able. But according to Ms. Michaels, this is not going to happen. And although Mrs. Ashburn hasn't been officially informed of this, we get the impression she suspects something.

"Well, my dress doesn't sound nearly as beautiful as yours," I tell her as she hands the paper cup back to me. Then to continue my distraction I describe my dress to her, saying how it looks a little bit like Audrey Hepburn, hoping she can relate to a movie icon that was part of her era.

"Oh my! That sounds very classic and elegant." She tells me about the "little black dress" she wore when her husband took her to New York for their fifteenth anniversary. "And Carl gave me a real string of pearls that year. It looked so lovely with the black dress. He actually took a photograph of me standing in front of Tiffany's." She chuckles. "As if I resembled Audrey Hepburn."

"I'll bet you did, too."

She frowns slightly. "I wonder where that photograph is . . ."

Then, to continue my distraction efforts, I ramble on a bit more about how my accessories won't be pearls but fake diamonds, and finally seeing that she's getting sleepy, I tell her good night and move on to help another resident. It's weird how much I can relate to old Mrs. Ashburn. It's like we've both been forced from our homes.

But at least she has a warm bed to sleep in.

On Friday morning I feel strangely energized. Like maybe I can pull this off for a while longer after all. Knowing I have a night off from work—not to mention going to the dance and everything else—well, I almost feel like I'm on top again. Like I might be able to survive my life.

Bristol seems oddly quiet in art. Lindsey and I make small talk, and I'm a bit surprised to hear that Lindsey is going to the dance too. For some reason, I assumed this librarian's helper had little or no life.

"Byron's just a friend of mine from youth group," Lindsey admits to me. "But I think it'll be fun just the same." Then she tells me about her dress. Something she and her mom found at a vintage shop, and it actually sounds very cool. I try not to feel envious to hear of a mom who's involved with her daughter like that.

"My dress is kind of vintage too," I say to Lindsey as I smooth the tip of my charcoal stick into a point.

"How so?" Bristol asks.

I'm surprised she's even been listening to us, but even more caught off guard by the frosty tone of her voice. As a result, I'm sharply reminded that I'm going to the very dance Bristol has been left out of . . . with the very guy she wishes she was going with. For me to talk about it like this, right in front of her, especially considering how exceptionally kind she's been to me lately, well, it's not very thoughtful on my part. I wish I could retract my entire conversation with Lindsey. What was I thinking?

"It's just a plain black dress," I say quickly, shrugging like Genevieve's favorite dress is simply an old rag. "Pretty basic, really." Then to change the subject, I ask Bristol about her drawing, lavishing what I hope sounds like sincere praise upon her.

But despite my efforts, she seems cool and distant now. I'm certain I must've offended her. I so wish I hadn't said anything about the dance. She's obviously jealous. Finally the bell rings, and since I've already packed up my things, I take off without even saying good-bye. I cannot get out of the art room soon enough.

"Hey, what's the big hurry?" Jayden jogs to catch up with me on my way to the cafeteria.

"Oh, sorry." I slow down for him. "I guess I'm just used to rushing around these days. It's like I'm on fast-speed or something."

"So . . . how's your mom doing now?"

"She's better. Fortunately, she's well enough to get moved to the nursing home now." As twisted as it sounds, I actually imagine a pale sick image of my mom resting in one of the beds at River Woods Care Center. It's like the lies are affecting my brain.

He smiles. "Good to hear."

"Yeah, it is. I mean, she's still really weak and her lungs are damaged, but she should recover . . . in time." I glance away from him, hating myself for this false world I've created. But really, what can I do?

"I feel so bad when I remember that night at your house." He pauses to open the door to the cafeteria. "You really seemed upset. And you had every reason to be, but I just didn't get how serious it was."

I nod, shoving the guilt down deeper inside of me, putting a lid on top. "Yeah, I think the whole thing took me by surprise too."

We get in line and are soon getting our food, which I still do not take for granted. In fact, I decide to splurge on the chef's salad today since my payday's not far off. Then we join the others at our table. Not surprisingly, everyone there seems to be talking about tonight's dance.

"Where's Bristol?" Lily asks.

Everyone glances around, but no one seems to know or care.

"I need to talk to her." Lily has her phone in hand now. "Garth Martin's my lab partner, and he just told me that Katie Lowell is really sick and now he's dateless for homecoming."

"So?" Isabella gives Lily a blank look.

"So . . . it's not like Garth and Katie are serious or anything; they were just going to the dance for fun. But Garth's already got his suit and everything, and he still wants to go. So I mentioned that Bristol is dateless too. And he asked me to ask her if she's interested in going."

"She won't be," Isabella tells Lily. "I know for a fact there's only one guy she would go to the dance with." Isabella tosses me a look that's partly sympathetic and partly smug. "But we know *that's* not going to happen." She smiles.

"Hey, Bristol," Lily says into her phone and steps away from the table so we don't catch the rest of her conversation.

"She won't go," Isabella says with confidence.

But when Lily returns to our table, she's wearing a catty smile. "Guess what?"

"Bristol is going with Garth?" I venture.

Lily nods victoriously, then sits back down.

"No way!" Isabella hits the table with her hand.

"*Way!* Although Bristol said we have to let Garth and her join our group or she won't go."

"No problem. We can fit four couples in the stretch Hummer," Ethan says.

"The more the merrier," Isabella says lightly, but I can tell by the glint in her eyes that she's curious. For that matter, so am I. Why would Bristol suddenly agree to go to the dance with Garth Martin? Not that Garth is a loser. He's actually quite nice. But it just doesn't add up.

"Where is Bristol anyway?" I ask Lily. "I mean, I just saw her in art last period, so I know she's in school."

"I'm not sure," Lily confesses. "She was acting kind of mysterious on the phone."

"Maybe she's off getting her dress," Caleb says.

Isabella laughs. "Yeah, right. She was off getting a dress even before she knew she had a date to the dance."

The conversation returns to tonight's plans and festivities, and Bristol and her mysterious absence are temporarily forgotten. Still, I feel uneasy knowing she'll be going with the rest of us to the dance. I actually looked forward to her absence. And Isabella's right. No matter who Bristol goes to the dance with, she'll probably still have her eye on Jayden. And despite how nice she's been lately—well, up until art class today—I still don't totally trust that girl.

Before lunch ends, I take Isabella aside. I've been slightly obsessing over how I can possibly get prepared for my big night inside my messy van. I've been haunted by images of me crawling out of Darth Vader with a piece of dirty laundry hanging from the back of my dress, my hair stringy, my makeup resembling something from a bad Halloween movie. Not only that, but to be picked up in the limo means I'll need to park the van at the condo and then what? Hang out in the bushes until my ride arrives? And what if the manager notices me there and gets suspicious?

"I want to put my hair in an up-do tonight." I carefully lay the foundation of my plan to Isabella. "But I'm not good with hair so I'm not really sure how to do it. If my mom wasn't sick, I'd ask her to help — "

"I know!" Isabella declares. "You bring your dress and everything to my house, and we'll both get ready there. My mom's great with hair. We'll get her to help you."

I hug her. "Thank you!"

"This is going to be the best night!" She pulls out her phone and immediately calls her mom, leaving a message and informing her of our plan. "It's all set."

I spend the rest of the afternoon trying to figure out how to get myself to Isabella's house after school — without parking Darth Vader there. No way do I want Isabella or her parents to see that horrible van sitting in front of their beautiful home. Finally, I decide my only option is to zip out to the van, gather up my dress and everything, and be all ready to catch a ride with Isabella right after school. And maybe, if I'm lucky, she'll ask me to spend the night at her house too. That would be heavenly!

"What's all that?" Isabella asks me when I meet up with her after school.

"My stuff for the dance," I explain slightly breathlessly. "I thought I was going to your house with you."

"Oh yeah." She nods eagerly. "So, you want to ride with me?"

"If you don't mind."

"Not at all." She glances around. "I still haven't seen Bristol this afternoon." She waves over to Lily. "Is Bristol around? Is she catching a ride home with you?"

"No." Lily closes her phone as she comes over to join us. "But that was her. She cut her last class and had her mom come get her so they could go dress shopping. Then she asked me to meet her at her house afterward, and we'll get ready there."

"Nothing like last minute." Isabella chuckles. "Hope the poor girl can find something decent to wear."

"Knowing Bristol, she will," Lily says with confidence.

Then we say good-bye and that we'll see them later and part ways. To my relief, Isabella is so consumed with her plans for giving us both facials with a new kit she recently got that she doesn't question why I wanted to ride home with her like this. And as soon as we're in her house, which looks even bigger and fancier than the last time I saw it — maybe because my house got so much smaller since then — she insists on seeing my dress and shoes. To my dismay, she doesn't seem quite as impressed with the dress as I had hoped.

"It's a nice dress," she says after examining it. "But when you said vintage, I assumed it was a designer, like Chanel or Gucci."

"Oh . . ." I sigh as I slip the plastic back over it.

Now she spies the red-soled shoes in my bag, letting out a small shriek of delight. "You got Christian Louboutin shoes!"

Fortunately I left the shoebox in the van, so it's not too obvious these are knockoffs. Still, I'm not sure whether I want to continue with this part of the charade or not. It's not like Isabella doesn't have a few imitations herself. And my life is so phony already, it would feel good to be honest about something. I seriously wonder if I'll ever know when or where to draw the line between fact and fiction again.

"These are absolutely gorgeous." Isabella kicks off her own shoes, then slips my black sandals on like they're made of gold. "And they fit me too." Now she's strutting around her oversized bedroom, checking herself out in her full-length mirror and practically drooling over my shoes. "Did you get these online too?"

I simply nod, deciding to just go with fiction. Really, in light of everything else, what's the difference? And fortunately she doesn't question the authenticity of these shoes. After we give each other facials and manicures, we spend even more time priming — and I actually start to feel a bit like a princess. Then Isabella's mom not only helps us with our hair but insists on taking lots of photos as we strike pose after pose in Isabella's bedroom. Isabella accuses her mother of hovering, but I like this attention. I like everything about this night. I'm having so much fun. I almost feel like I'm someone else.

"What are you wearing to keep you warm?" Mrs. Marx asks me.

"Good question." Isabella goes into her oversized walk-in closet, then emerges wearing a furry silver jacket. "Check this out. Mom's letting me use my grandmother's old mink."

"Real mink?" I reach over to touch the incredibly soft fur.

"I had to get it out of cold storage," Mrs. Marx explains. "But I thought, why not? Still, I'm worried about you, Adele." She touches my bare arm. "You'll be freezing out there tonight."

I shrug. "I guess I hadn't even thought of that."

"I have this little black cape," Mrs. Marx says suddenly. "It's an old Ralph Lauren I've had since Isabella was a baby."

"Yes!" Isabella exclaims. "That cape would be perfect."

And just like that, Mrs. Marx exits and within minutes

returns with a lovely black velvet cape lined with luxurious satin.

"This is so nice," I say as she slips it over my shoulders. "Are you sure you don't mind loaning it to me?"

She just laughs. "Absolutely. Really, it's indestructible."

Isabella nods to affirm this. "I've heard that, as a baby, I threw up all over it on our way home from my grandparents' once."

I look nervously down at the cape.

"Don't worry, it's been cleaned since then," Mrs. Marx assures me as she leaves Isabella and me standing in front of the mirror admiring our grown-up-looking selves.

"What about a purse?" I ask Isabella.

Isabella holds up a small beaded evening bag. "Mom loaned this to me, but I don't really want to carry it around. I mean, I'll probably just end up losing it." She frowns. "But I should probably take my phone and lip gloss."

"Do you want me to carry the bag for you?"

She sticks her hand into what appears to be a pocket tucked into the side of her fur coat with a surprised expression. "Hey, this will work." She slips her phone and lip gloss into the pocket and grins. "Perfect."

I check the cape to discover it has no pockets.

"Don't worry," Isabella assures me. "We'll just share the lip gloss, and if we need a phone, which seems unlikely, I've got mine. That way we'll both travel light."

"Cool." I toss my phone back with my other stuff. "My phone's almost dead anyway."

And as if Mrs. Marx hasn't been generous enough already, she's also prepared a bunch of appetizers and things for us downstairs. Then to my surprise, as we're waiting for the guys to arrive, Isabella's dad opens a bottle of real champagne and offers us both a small glass to celebrate our big night. I honestly feel like I'm starring in one of the *Princess Diary* movies—like this is all a sweet dream. But it's real. And despite my usual undercurrent of uneasiness, I wish this night could just go on and on. I even imagine that it can. Maybe Isabella's parents will decide to adopt me tomorrow morning.

It's around six thirty when Ethan and Jayden arrive, and Isabella's mom poses us by the staircase, taking even more photos. The guys eat some of the appetizers, although no champagne is offered to them. And then it's time to go and pick up the others. As we're walking out to where an elegant white stretch Hummer is parked in the circular driveway, Jayden takes my hand and whispers in my ear, "You look absolutely beautiful tonight, Adele."

I thank him and compliment him on his suit. Then, like a perfect gentleman, he helps me into the limo. I feel so very grown up and unbelievably happy . . . and somewhat unreal. But it's good . . . very good. The other guys, Garth and Caleb, are already in the limo, and then we're off to pick up the other girls, who are waiting at Bristol's house only a few blocks away. I've never been to Bristol's before, but I'm not too surprised to see that it's higher up the hill than Isabella's. And it's bigger and fancier too.

As the Hummer pulls into the long driveway, we discuss whether we should all go in, but Ethan checks the time and decides that we should let Caleb and Garth get the other girls so we can get moving and make it to the restaurant to secure our reservation. This is a relief to me since I don't really want to go inside Bristol's house. And although I'm trying to think positively, I really don't look forward to seeing Bristol tonight. I have a feeling that Jayden feels the same as he takes my hand in his and gives it a warm squeeze.

Of course, both Bristol and Lily look gorgeous. Lily's dress is creamy white satin, trimmed with rhinestones. But, oddly enough, Bristol has on a little black dress that's not much different than mine. I'm not sure whether to be dismayed or flattered because I know Bristol heard me describing my dress during art, so it can't be a coincidence. And considering how Isabella wanted our dresses to be complementary to each other, I'm curious as to her reaction but am relieved she's not mentioning it. So I will try to ignore this little irritation too. At least I'm the girl with Jayden!

Our group makes pleasant small talk as we are transported in style across town. And I'm not sure if it's my imagination or not, but Bristol seems unusually quiet and cool. However, once we're at the restaurant waiting to be seated, it's as if she's become the life of the party. She is pleasant and cheerful to everyone. Even me. And as we're led to our table, she insists we sit in boy-girl order, and naturally, she manages to snag the seat next to Jayden. Still, I don't care. I know that Jayden has no interest in her.

Dinner goes relatively smoothly, but for some reason I feel like my guard is up with Bristol. I'm not even sure why since she's actually being exceptionally nice. Maybe it's because she's being so nice, so sweet and complimentary to everyone . . . especially Jayden. Or maybe I'm just paranoid.

"So, who do you think will win homecoming queen this year?" Lily says as a decadent chocolate dessert is being served. Now, we're all well aware that Isabella's name is on the ballot. But Isabella didn't campaign and she played the whole thing down, so much so that I nearly forgot. No one even expects her to win.

"I think Emily Hershey has this one in the bag," Isabella

proclaims. "I even voted for her myself."

"You mean you didn't vote for yourself?" Ethan says.

She just laughs. "Of course not, silly. I don't want to be queen."

"Well, I think you have a serious chance," Bristol tells her. "I voted for you."

Now everyone else at the table admits they voted for Isabella as well. I say the same thing, although it's another lie. The truth is, I was so distracted with my life that I forgot to vote. And my guess is that Emily Hershey will probably win. I even stopped by one of her campaign tables for a free chocolate bar last week. But to be fair I was hungry that day. Even so, I act like Isabella has a chance.

Bristol holds up her water glass like she's about to make a toast. "Here's to Bella — no matter what the outcome is tonight, she's still our queen."

Everyone follows suit, saying, "Here's to Queen Isabella!"

Isabella is beaming. "Well, even if I don't win, and I don't expect to, you guys are all very sweet."

Bristol is earning a lot of brownie points tonight. And not just with Isabella either. It's like everyone at the table, even Jayden, is warming up to her. And for some reason this is making me very uncomfortable. Maybe I'm imagining things, but something about this does not feel right.

When we're back in the Hummer on our way to the hotel where the dance is being held, Bristol turns her attention to me. "Well, Adele, it looks like we could pass for sisters tonight," she says in a voice that, to my ears, sounds coated with saccharine.

"You two do look a bit alike," Lily agrees. "Same hair color. And your dresses are really similar and—"

"Mine's just a Valentino," Bristol says. "Tonight was such short notice that my mom actually borrowed it from a friend of hers, then had some quick alterations done so it would fit me."

I nod. "It's very pretty."

"What's your dress?" Bristol asks. "Let me guess . . ." She frowns slightly as she looks at it. "Hmm . . . I'm not sure."

"Chanel?" ventures Lily with what almost seems like a wicked glimmer in her eye, like she knows it's nothing special.

"No . . ." I glance out the window where the blur of car lights zips past us in the opposite direction. "I'm not really sure who made it."

"You didn't even look at the label?" Bristol looks stunned.

"What is it with some girls and designers?" Jayden wrinkles his nose in disgust. "Who cares whose name is on a label anyway? What's the big deal? I think Adele looks like a million bucks."

I smile at him. "Thanks."

"Oh, it's not *that* big of a deal," Bristol says quickly. "It's just that *some* people pretend to be wearing designers . . . you know, putting on pretenses and acting like they're something they're not."

"Wannabes and posers," Lily says in a superior way. "I can't stand them."

Bristol nods. "I personally find it irritating when people attempt to pass themselves off like that. I can't stand phonies." She's staring directly at me now. "How about you, Adele? Do you like phonies?"

I swallow hard and try to think of a response.

"Well, her dress might not be a designer," Isabella says, "but did you see her shoes?"

Bristol just shrugs.

Isabella points to my feet. "Check them out. Christian Louboutin. I told Adele to watch out because I might resort to some shoe-snatching before the night is over."

"They're not *real* Christian Louboutin." The way Bristol says this is confusing. I'm not sure if she's making a statement or asking a question. All I know is this is not good.

"Yes," Isabella declares on my behalf. "Check out those red soles. They're the real deal. I already tried them on and they're delicious."

"I'd like to check them out." Bristol nods at me like she expects me to stick my foot up in the air. Perhaps in her face, which I wouldn't mind doing just now. Instead, I simply force a very stiff smile.

"Well?" she says, like she's waiting for me to do something.

"Let's see the soles of your shoes, Adele."

I gracefully raise my foot to reveal the red sole beneath the pretty shoe and then, feeling worried, quickly put it back down.

"Let's see that shoe again." Bristol clicks on the overhead light, which really brightens the interior of the limo.

"Man, Bristol." Jayden frowns at her. "You need to get out more, girl."

"I just want a better look," Bristol says in a cheery voice. "You know how we girls are about shoes."

Hoping to get this over with, since it looks like we're almost to the hotel, I lift my foot again. Only this time, Bristol actually grabs my ankle, lifting the shoe to expose the red sole better. And then she laughs. "Just as I suspected."

"What?" I stare at her as she drops my foot so it lands with a dull thud.

"Fake." She nods with satisfaction as the limo pulls in front of the hotel. "Just like you."

"Bristol!" Isabella shakes a finger at her. "Don't act like such a—"

"Sorry." Bristol makes an innocent face. "But I just have a serious problem with fakes."

"What do you mean?" Isabella demands. "Adele is *not* a fake."

"Oh yes, she is, and I can prove it." Bristol's eyes are locked on me now. In fact, everyone's eyes seem to be on me. I wish we could just get out of this car and get on with the dance and forget any of this happened, but it's like a bad dream that refuses to end.

"Knock it off, Bristol," Jayden firmly tells her. "No one is amused."

"I'm surprised at you." She turns to Jayden. "You of all

people . . . I thought you hated fakes even more than I do."

"Adele is not a fake." He reaches for my hand. "Let's go."

"Wait a minute," Bristol says. "At least you can hear the truth."

"From you?" Jayden frowns at Bristol.

"Then hear it from Adele." Bristol points her finger at me. "Why don't you just tell everyone what's really going on with you. Admit that your mom isn't sick and in the hospital. Tell us all about how your mom lost her job and how you guys got evicted from your condo and how you've been just playing all of us for a bunch of fools."

"Bristol Louise Allen," exclaims Isabella, "you have totally lost your mind."

"You seriously need to get over yourself, Bristol," Ethan adds. "This is not funny."

"And quit picking on Adele." Jayden is tugging on my hand now, trying to get me to stand up and exit the limo with him, but it's like I'm stuck to the leather seat, like my legs won't move.

"Don't let her get to you," Isabella tells me. "We should've known she'd pull a stunt like this."

Bristol just shrugs. "Hey, sometimes the truth hurts. But you don't have to shoot the messenger."

"You're totally nuts, Bristol." Jayden shakes his head as he pulls on my hand again. Somehow I manage to stand and get out of the limo with him helping to steady me. But my legs feel like rubber as Jayden guides me into the hotel. And then the beef medallions I just had for dinner begin doing somersaults in my stomach. So much so I'm afraid I might actually hurl all over the beautiful Oriental carpet of the posh hotel lobby.

"Excuse me," I say to Jayden. "I need to visit the ladies' room." He nods and I rush off in search of a bathroom or any place I can hide and attempt to figure this thing out. Part of me just wants to confess everything—get it out in the open and over with, admit that Bristol is right, and accept the consequences. Another part of me wants to stand up to Bristol and deny everything. And I almost think I could make it seem like she's really the devil in disguise by picking on a girl whose mother is possibly dying right now. And yet another part of me wants to play the kicked dog, tuck my tail between my legs, and just tear out of this place.

"Are you okay?" Isabella asks as she finds me in the ladies' room where I'm standing in front of a sink just staring at my image in the mirror, wondering who am I and how did I get here?

I shake my head, blinking to hold back the tears.

"I don't understand Bristol." Isabella puts a hand on my shoulder. "For a while she was being so nice, just like she used to be. Then totally out of the blue she launches this major attack on you. It's seriously deranged. I honestly think Bristol is losing it."

I press my lips together and nod. I have no words. No defense. No answers.

"I feel so bad that we even let her come with us," Isabella continues. "And I really don't know why she's acting like—"

"I'll tell you why Bristol is acting like this." Bristol is directly behind me now. I never even saw her come in. "Because Bristol is telling the truth."

Now Lily is behind Bristol too. All of us are looking at our reflections in the mirror. Four girls, dressed for a dance. It should've been such a delightful evening . . . but it's all gone sideways.

"Isabella," Lily says, "you'd better listen to Bristol."

"*Why?*" Isabella's forehead creases.

"Because she *is* telling the truth."

"Oh, Lily!" Isabella looks angry. "I cannot believe you'd take Bristol's side. This was supposed to be such a fun evening, and it's like you're determined to ruin everything. Honestly, what is wrong with you?"

"Listen to me." Lily puts both hands on Isabella's shoulders. "I was *with* Bristol when she went to Westwood Heights this afternoon to get to the bottom of this. I witnessed her talking to—"

"*What?*" Isabella looks stunned. "What on earth are you guys doing snooping around like that? It's like I don't even know you two."

"Listen!" Lily says again. "I'll admit I was skeptical when Bristol asked me to drive her to Adele's house, but then I saw and heard it all for myself. Bristol actually talked to the manager there, and unless he is lying, which is ridiculous, what Bristol is telling you about Adele and her mom is true."

"Why are you sneaking around asking questions about Adele in the first place?" Isabella points her finger at Bristol. "Just because Jayden likes her instead of you? I am so sick of it. Why can't you just get over your obsession? Instead you have to spoil everything for everyone!"

"It's not like that." Bristol shakes her head. "I swear! It's just that nothing made sense. First Lindsey Nelson talking about how Adele was spending all this time at the public library. Then I saw Adele getting into this weird-looking black van and—"

"What?" Isabella looks thoroughly confused.

"So I decided to visit Adele at the condo. And that's when I saw an eviction notice on their door."

"I don't believe it," Isabella declares.

"It's true," Lily tells her. "I saw it myself."

"Maybe you were at the wrong condo," Isabella says with a slight waver in her voice, tossing me a worried glance like she is starting to buy into this. And why shouldn't she?

"I thought so too," Bristol says. "And I was concerned. So Lily and I went to the manager's office, and he told us that Adele and her mom had been evicted a couple of weeks ago for not paying their rent."

Isabella looks truly shocked now. As do the two girls who just came in here to check their lip gloss but quickly left after Bristol gave them one of her looks.

"And I checked all the local hospitals," Bristol continues. "Adele's mother isn't in any of them. And she never was. All of it, everything that Adele told us, was a complete and total lie."

I want to defend myself but don't even know where to begin. I consider questioning why a hospital would give out information about a patient, but knowing Bristol, I'm sure she has her ways. Besides, what difference does it make now? Really, most of what she's saying is the truth. And more than ever, I know the truth hurts.

"So all this while," Bristol continues in a calm but deadly tone, "Adele has been playing on our sympathies. She's carried out this act—that her poor sick mother is on the verge of death. Consequently, we've all been supportive and sweet to her. Just swallowing up all of her poisoned lies like candy. But the truth is, she and her mom really were evicted for not paying their bills."

"Not only that," Lily chimes in, "but the manager said that Adele's mom was a drug dealer too."

"That's a lie," I say in a raspy voice.

"That's exactly what the manager told us," Bristol says to me. "He also said that you and your mom left the place in a big mess and that there was drug paraphernalia all over and that he's already informed the police."

"That's right," Lily declares. "I heard it myself." She turns to Isabella and puts a comforting hand on her shoulder. "I don't know about you, but I feel used, Isabella. And I do not like being lied to. It makes me feel dirty just knowing someone like Adele Porter claimed to be our friend. I can just imagine how she probably laughed behind our backs as she pulled this whole thing over on us."

"I can't believe how we fell for her tricks and trusted her," Bristol says coldly. "I thought we were smarter than that."

"And have you considered how this could impact our college acceptances?" Lily asks Isabella. "Or how your college board would react if they knew you were friends with a con artist?"

"Or a drug dealer?" Bristol adds. "For all we know, Adele and her mom might've hoped to make us into their drug clients. They obviously knew we could afford it."

I want to die right now. I wish the white marble floor would crack open and just swallow me whole. I wouldn't fight or complain.

Isabella turns to me with a pained look, like I have intentionally hurt her. "Is this true?"

"It's not like she's painting it," I say weakly.

*"Is it true?"* Isabella demands. "Have you been lying to all of us? After we welcomed you into our circle of friends, have you simply been using us? Pretending to be someone you're not?"

"You don't understand. It's hard to explain, but if you'll just listen—"

"We're sick of listening to your lies," Bristol tells me, then she points down to my feet. "You're a fake, Adele Porter. Just like your shoes."

## CHAPTER 12

The expression on Isabella's face was enough to convince me it's over. Her hurt and disappointment were the final twist to the knife Bristol had stuck into my back. And I knew that my short-lived stint as one of them was over. So without saying a word, I turned away and walked out of the bathroom, out of the hotel, and I just kept on going.

I suppose I had hoped that someone would chase after me and stop me. Maybe even Jayden, although I don't think he saw me leave. Or if he did, he pretended not to. And I'm sure he's heard the whole story by now anyway. At first I walked slowly, hoping that perhaps Isabella would rethink her harsh dismissal of me and feel guilty. Maybe she'd even apologize or ask if there was some way to help me, but no one came to check on me.

So, as usual, I am on my own. And really, isn't this what I deserve? But as I continue walking aimlessly down the busy street, I grow painfully aware of two things. First of all, these fake Christian Louboutins are crippling. Second of all, I have no place to stay tonight. Right now my purse, with my van keys and all my money and my cell phone, is in Isabella's bedroom. And short of hitchhiking, I have no way to get back there tonight. To say this is freaky is a huge understatement.

I pass by a coffee shop and consider stopping in to give my poor feet a rest and attempt to figure out my problems, except I have no money for a cup of coffee. I even consider panhandling, but I'm afraid I'll be mistaken as a hooker in my sequined dress and fake diamonds.

"Hey, good looking," a guy calls out from across the street. "What'cha doing tonight? Wanna go to a party?"

Ignoring his skanky invitation — not the first one I've received — I suddenly realize I've actually wandered into what is known as the "bad side of town." Common sense says to turn around and walk in the opposite direction, but my feet are killing me and there's no way I'll return to that hotel to face my "friends." Besides, I know now that they were never really my friends. It was simply a game I'd been playing. A game I couldn't possibly win. For a "smart" girl, I've been incredibly stupid these past few weeks.

I walk a bit farther, just to get away from the party-invite dude, and finally when my feet can't take another step, I sit on a cement bench by the bus stop. I have never felt so lost . . . so alone. The cold of the bench seeps into me as I stare into the traffic moving along the street. People with lives, going places, riding in cars, on their way to somewhere — it all feels so foreign to me now. Like I'm an alien visiting from another planet. Like I've been plunked down here to observe, but all I feel is a vast kind of empty loneliness . . . like there is no hope . . . like I will always be on the outside of everything.

Finally, I can't take it. The idea of jumping out in front of one of the fast-moving vehicles, like the big UPS truck whizzing by, suddenly becomes very appealing. I watch as the headlights and taillights whoosh by me. I try to imagine whether or not I would feel anything when I was struck. Would it hurt? Or would it happen so fast—a quick end to all this suffering—that I would feel nothing?

I wonder about my so-called friends. If they heard about my tragic demise in the news, would they feel sorry or guilty? More than likely, they wouldn't even care. Or perhaps they'd simply chalk it up to the result of my imposter lifestyle, saying "she got what she deserved."

Maybe my mom would be sad . . . at least I hope she would. That is, if she ever discovered what happened to me. And hopefully she'd feel guilty too. Because isn't this whole mess her fault too? Doesn't she bear some responsibility for this tragedy . . . my so-called life? I lean over now, burying my face in my hands, letting the tears flow freely. I cry until my throat burns and my head throbs. Over and over I ask myself, what am I going to do? *What am I going to do?*

After a while, I'm sure my tears are all spent, and I sit up straight and take in a deep breath. I wipe my wet cheeks with the backs of my hands. I am not a quitter. I am a fighter . . . a survivor . . . and I will not give up.

"Are you all right?"

I look up to see an elderly woman gazing down at me with gentle eyes. At least I think she's an old woman. But as I study her more closely, I realize she's probably more like middle-aged or even my mom's age. And she smells of strong alcohol.

I kind of shrug. "Yeah . . . I'm okay."

"Why were you crying?" She sits beside me, and sticking her hands in the pockets of an oversized coat, she peers curiously at me.

I sigh, wondering if I should just make something up. But at the same time, I'm so sick of lies. As painful as tonight has been, there is a tiny spark of relief in knowing that my web of lies has finally come to an end.

"Why are you all dressed up?" She frowns at me. "You a *working girl?*"

I consider this. Does she really think I'm a prostitute?

"I'm warning you, this is Marla's street, and if you think you're gonna work here, you better talk to Marla first, 'cuz I've seen that girl get mad. And it ain't a pretty sight neither."

I firmly shake my head. "I am *not* a hooker."

"That's a good thing, 'cuz take it from me, it'll kill you for sure. I know more girls who go down that road and never come back. It's a dead-end street if you ask me."

I pull Isabella's mother's velvet cape more closely around me. Somehow I need to get this garment back to her, all in one piece and in good shape. And I need to get the dress back to Genevieve too. For some reason these two things feel important to me.

"So, why are you all dressed up then?" she persists.

With nothing to hide, I simply uncork the bottle of my life and pour out the whole story for her. All of it. From how my mom abandoned me, to my rich friends and my phony life, to living in a van and working in a nursing home. I get clear to this evening and how my purse and keys and cell phone are all stuck in my ex-friend's house.

"Why don't you just go get your stuff? Your purse and belongings, why not just go get them?"

I consider this.

"It's your stuff, ain't it?"

I nod.

"Then you go get it. I'm telling you, if you don't stand up for yourself and your own stuff, no one else will." Then she launches into a story about how her ex-boyfriend took all her belongings while she was gone one day and how he never gave anything back. And while her story is different from mine, what she's saying makes sense. Unfortunately, I don't have a clue as to how to do this.

She pulls a bottle out from inside her coat, unscrews the lid, takes a swig, then holds the bottle out to me like she thinks I'd like some too.

"No thank you." I force a smile. "I'm not a drinker."

She shakes a dirty finger in my face. "Not yet you ain't. But trust me, you will be. You stay out here like this . . . and you will be."

I want to argue this point, but it's pointless. Besides, this woman's been a good listener tonight. I stick out my hand to her. "My name's Adele."

She puts the bottle back inside her coat, then takes my hand and shakes it. "Nice to meet ya, Adele. My name's Dolly. Just like Dolly Parton." She grins and pats her chest. "Except I ain't exactly endowed like Ms. Parton." She chuckles. "She's got more money too."

I just nod, still wondering what I should do tonight.

"If you need help, you should go to the mission."

"The mission?"

She tips her head on down the street. "Couple blocks that way. They got food and beds and they *say* they want to help folks." She lets out a loud cackle of a laugh. "Except you gotta *pay* for their help."

"They expect you to pay?" I frown. "What if you're broke?"

"You don't pay in money." She shakes her head. "No, you pay with your ears. You gotta listen to the preacher do his preaching."

"Oh . . ."

She nods as she reaches into her coat and removes the bottle again, taking another long swig.

"Do you stay there?"

She shakes her head as she replaces the bottle. "Nope. Not me."

"Why not?"

"They check your clothes." She grins to reveal a set of darkened teeth. "I don't go where my bottle ain't welcome."

"So, where do you stay?"

"Here and there." She stands slowly to her feet, wobbling a bit from side to side. "And that's where I'm going now."

"Take care, Dolly."

"You too." She looks puzzled. "What's your name again, girl?"

"Adele."

She smiles. "Pretty name . . . pretty girl. You take care too, Adele." Then she slowly staggers back in the direction I just came from. I stand too. But instead of walking back toward the hotel, I head the other way. If there really is a mission, I want to find out just what kind of help they really can offer. After a couple of blocks, my feet are throbbing again, and I'm wondering if Dolly got her directions mixed up. But after a couple more blocks, I see a lit-up sign that says Jesus Saves! I have no idea what that's supposed to mean, but my feet are so sore that I intend to find out. Maybe Jesus can save me from being permanently crippled by these brutal shoes.

"I'm sorry," a man tells me as he opens the door. "Dinner is over, miss."

"I'm not here for dinner." I study him, trying to determine what sort of role he plays here. He doesn't exactly strike me as a bum. But then how would I know? He has short gray hair, is cleanly shaved and neatly dressed. A number of other people of various ages are milling about in what seems to be a dining room behind him. And judging by their raggedy and unkempt appearances, I'm guessing they actually do belong here.

I can tell by this man's creased brow that he's trying to figure me out too. "Are you here to volunteer then?" he asks cheerfully.

I force a small smile. "I wish I were, but the truth is I need help."

He nods. "What kind of help?"

I press my lips together. Is this a big mistake? What if someone here tries to turn me in to Children's Services for being underage? Maybe they have a legal responsibility to do something like that.

"Are you a prostitute?" he asks in a surprisingly gentle tone.

I can't believe I've been asked this twice in one night, not to mention the proposition from the party dude. But then I figure it must be due to my slightly glitzy outfit, that and being out on the streets alone. I will not take it personally.

"No, I'm a homeless person who was trying to pretend to be something she's not. But it didn't work out too well."

He nods in a knowing way. "I'm Pastor Roland. Why don't we go to my office and talk?"

I follow Pastor Roland to a small office, and he leaves the door open. I can hear the others milling about where I noticed one of the long tables was set up with coffee and fresh fruit. "Let's start with your name," he suggests.

"Adele."

His eyes light up. "Really?"

I'm not sure how to respond. Does he think I'm lying? "Yes. My name is really Adele." I purposely leave off my last name for fear he might turn me in to the authorities.

He smiles now. "Adele was my wife's name."

"Oh . . ." I nod. "Was?"

"She died about nine years ago. That's one reason I've been volunteering here. Helps to fill some lonely nights for me. So tell me, Adele, what brings you here tonight?"

For the second time, I spill the beans. And everything I say is true . . . well, except for my age. I would be honest about this, but I just can't risk getting stuck in foster care again.

"But you see, I do have a job and I plan to save up enough to rent something cheap—maybe just a room. It's just that I'm kind of stuck tonight. If I could just get my things from my friend's house, I'll be all right. The main thing is, I cannot miss going to work tomorrow." I sigh. "Without my job . . . I'm sunk."

He seems relieved. "That's simple enough. I can give you a ride on my way home. My shift ends at nine." He glances at the clock on the wall. "And that's less than thirty minutes."

Suddenly I feel a rush of apprehension. Do I really want to get into a car with a stranger? This goes against everything I've been taught since childhood. And yet, what are my options here? To wander the streets dressed like a hooker?

"But first I need to put away the coffee things," he tells me as he stands.

"Want any help?"

"Sure." He grins. "I never refuse help."

As I help him put away the coffee things, which for some reason must be locked in a cabinet, he talks to me about his volunteer job here at the mission. As it turns out, a number of the local pastors take turns working here. "I volunteer on Fridays," he tells me as we wipe down the kitchen countertops. "I come here in the morning, do a bit of counseling during the day, then I give the sermon at dinner."

"Oh, yeah, I heard that's how people pay for their meals here," I say as I recall Dolly's warning.

He chuckles. "I suppose that's what it feels like to some of my listeners. Truth is, it's a nice setup for me, too. I always practice the sermon I plan to give on the following Sunday. Not that the crowd is the same exactly. But in some ways, they're not that much different."

Before long it's nine and I no longer feel worried about this man's character. Just being around him, hearing him react to others, watching them interact with him . . . I think I'm totally safe. Still, as we're driving across town in his musty-smelling older sedan, I'm a little uneasy. But I think it's related to everything that's gone down tonight. It's like my brain is getting fuzzy, and it's all starting to feel a little surreal.

"Your friend must be quite wealthy," he says as he pulls up in front of Isabella's big house.

"Her parents seem to be."

"And have you thought about living with them?"

I just shake my head. "I'm pretty sure this girl isn't really my friend anymore, not after what happened tonight."

"Too bad." He sighs. "That's what I'd call a fair-weather friend."

I shrug and reach for the door handle.

"Now, you want me to wait for you, right? And take you to where your van is parked?"

I study his face. He really does have kind eyes. And yet I've heard that some sociopaths do too. Is it possible this sweet old guy will drive down some lonely road and slit my throat? On the other hand, I can't exactly walk back to the high school. Still, if I'm going to do this—survive on my own—I need to be street smart.

"I suppose my friend's parents will offer me a ride," I say in what I hope sounds like an offhand way and not an outright lie. "But I'll just tell them I'd rather have a ride with you."

As I walk up to the house, I realize I probably sounded pretty lame, but it makes me feel better, like I'm warning Pastor Roland, if he really is a pastor, that someone knows where I am tonight . . . who I'm with.

But even more nerve-wracking than imagining I'm riding around town with an old sociopath is having to ring the doorbell to Isabella's house. My knees are literally shaking as Mr. Marx opens the door. I'm not even sure I can speak or what I will say.

"Adele?" His face creases with worry. "What are you doing here? Is something wrong? Are you girls okay?"

"Not exactly. I mean, don't worry, Isabella's fine," I say quickly. "Something happened . . . and, well, I just needed to leave the dance early. Anyway, I wanted to pick up my things."

He still looks confused. "You're not spending the night with Isabella?"

"No. Something came up. I'm sorry to disturb you like this. But my ride is waiting." I jerk my thumb back to where Pastor Roland's old car is parked. Like me, it looks so out of place in this upscale neighborhood. "If you don't mind, I'll just get my things and go."

"Sure. Come in." He still looks puzzled and perhaps even a bit suspicious as he lets me in.

"I'll just be a minute." I hurry up the stairs. I can hear him coming behind me. Probably to make sure I don't steal the silver or the family jewels.

"Did something bad happen at the dance?" He follows me to Isabella's room.

I turn and look directly at him. "Yes."

He looks totally taken aback at this. *"What?"*

"Everyone found out that I'm a fraud."

His dark brows draw together. "A fraud?"

I nod as I gather up my bag, carelessly stuffing my school clothes and other items into it.

"I don't understand."

I can feel him watching me, but I don't look up as I sit on Isabella's bed, removing the dreadful knockoff shoes and replacing them with my favorite Frye boots. I'm sure this must look strange with my glitzy dress, but I no longer care.

"What do you mean . . . a fraud?" Mr. Marx presses a bit further.

"Yes, that's what I am," I say calmly, like it's really no big deal. "I was pretending to be like them, one of them. But clearly I am not."

"One of whom?"

I stand and look evenly at him now. "You know . . . one of the lucky ones. The wellborn elite. But we can't really help it if we're from the wrong side of the tracks, if we're born into the wrong families, can we?"

He looks even more perplexed as he slowly shakes his head. "No, I don't suppose you can help it."

I remove his wife's black velvet cape, carefully smoothing it out as I lay it down on Isabella's bed. "Please tell your wife thank you for the use of her lovely cape. And please tell Isabella I'm very, very sorry."

He looks like he wants to say something more, but no words find their way past his thin, pursed lips. And it's just as well. I pull my jacket on over my little black dress, then push past him, hurrying down the stairs, out the door, and back into Pastor

Roland's musty old car, which to my surprise feels much more comfortable than it did on the way over here. Despite that, there's a lump in my throat and I feel close to tears again. I am grateful for the silence as he drives toward the high school.

"You seem like a sensible girl to me." Pastor Roland turns onto the street where the school is located. "And I suspect you'll land on your feet. But if you ever need help again, please remember the mission. It's not perfect, but it's better than the streets."

"Thanks. I'll keep that in mind."

He reaches into his pocket and pulls out what looks like a business card. "And our church likes to help out people too." He hands me the card. "Feel free to come visit us if you like. Perhaps this Sunday."

"Thanks. I'll think about it." I point to Darth Vader. "That's my van over there."

"And you were honest with me, Adele? You really do have a job at River Woods Care Center?"

"Absolutely." I even tell him my hours and the name of my supervisor.

"And they really don't mind you parking the van there until you find a permanent place to live?"

I consider my answer. I know I tried to paint this a little different than the truth, the whole truth, and nothing but the truth. But what if he knows someone at River Woods? Perhaps it's best to just put my cards on the table and hope he is trustworthy. "To be honest, they don't actually know I've been sleeping in my van. But really, it's only a temporary setup. I do plan to find a better place — just as soon as I can. I mean, after all, winter isn't far off. I know I can't stay in the van forever."

He nods, but I can tell he's not totally convinced.

"I'm sure my mom will be back soon. If not, I'll rent a room or a cheap apartment. I appreciate your concern, but really, I'm fine."

He smiles. "Okay. But remember if you ever need help, our church members might be old, but we're a friendly bunch."

I thank him again. Then with my backpack in hand, I get out and wave good-bye. As I put the key into the driver's door, I cannot believe how thoroughly happy I am to see this ugly black van. It's like I want to give old Darth Vader a great big hug. I get in and start the engine, and with Pastor Roland's car following behind me, almost as if he wants to be sure I'm really doing what I said I would do, I turn down the street and drive toward River Woods. When he sees me turn in there, he continues on his way.

I let out a sigh of relief as I park on the edge of the employee parking section. Now I have no doubt that Pastor Roland is a decent man. Yet at the same time, I'm aware that I've divulged enough information to get myself into trouble. His concern about me living in a van was genuine. But what if he suspects I'm younger than eighteen? What will happen if he calls the state and turns me in?

Still, I decide not to think about that tonight. I am emotionally and physically exhausted and almost too tired to care. Feeling like the Cinderella who never even got to go to the ball, I am grateful for Darth Vader's creepy tinted windows as I carefully remove Genevieve's little black dress, hang it on the hanger, and wrap it in the rumpled plastic.

As I pull on sweats, I am determined to pay for the dry-cleaning I know the dress will need. But right now, all I want to do is crash in the back of my van and sleep for a long, long time. Or at least until ten thirty tomorrow morning when it will be time to get up and get ready for work. I can't believe I'm relieved to know I'll be cleaning up after smelly old people — unless Bristol does something to sabotage that for me.

## CHAPTER 13

The only thing more pathetic than hanging gaudy Halloween decorations in a nursing home is my life. Seriously. It was exceedingly sad last night and it doesn't look much better today. The icing on my flattened cake was waking up in the back of a van with the scratched-up red soles of my "Christian Louboutin" shoes staring me in the face—and realizing that I paid $49.99 for those torturous heels. Fifty bucks wasted! Just shoot me!

"I think it needs to be a little lower, Adele." Genevieve looks up from the safety of the dayroom floor.

I adjust the green-faced broom-riding cardboard witch down the column several inches. "Better?"

"Now the residents can actually see it."

"You don't think it'll scare them?" I ask with concern.

Genevieve laughs. "Scare them? It kind of *resembles* them."

"Very funny," Ellen says as she comes around a corner with the med cart.

"Sorry." Genevieve gives me an apologetic smile, then scurries away.

"You better be careful up there," Ellen warns me. "We don't want any workers' comp suits here."

With my masking tape roll "bracelet," I finish adhering the witch to the column, then cautiously get down from the plastic chair I've been perched on. "I couldn't find a stepladder." I nod toward the plastic crate of Halloween decorations. "And Ms. Michaels asked me to put these things up today."

Now she smiles at me. "And Ms. Michaels tells me that you've been promoted from the kitchen."

"Yes. She just hired someone else to help Mary." I try not to look too relieved since Ellen and Scary Mary actually get along.

"We noticed that you handle yourself well among the residents, and it seems a number of them feel quite comfortable with you. So it seems a nice promotion."

I want to add that it would be even nicer if the "promotion" came with a raise but think better of this.

"Just be careful when you're climbing around on things," she warns me as she continues on her way. "No broken bones."

Imagining what a mess my life would be if I did get hurt, I am careful, watching my step as I tape cats, pumpkins, and witches around the nursing home. Still, I'm a bit concerned that some residents won't like emerging from their rooms to discover spiders and bats have invaded their "happy" home. However, no one really seems to notice. Or like me, they just don't care.

"So I'm dying to know," Genevieve says as soon as we sit down for a soda during our afternoon break, "how was your big night?"

I let out a groan. "Don't ask."

Of course, this only makes her push harder. And finally I just dump the whole ugly story on her, and she is genuinely shocked. "You're kidding!"

I shake my head and take a sip of soda.

"Oh, Adele, that's absolutely horrible. You really went to the mission?"

"Don't worry, your dress is okay. But I'll pay to have it cleaned."

"No you won't. Not after the awful night you had."

"I want to," I tell her.

"No way. You've suffered enough." Now she winks at me. "But if it'll make you feel any better, I'll let you help Bess with dinner tonight."

"Bess on a Saturday night." I sigh to think of the poor senile resident who can barely eat and hardly responds to anything. "How much better does it get?"

Genevieve narrows her eyes. "So . . . you're really homeless then?"

Okay, this is one part I wish I'd left out of my little confession. I wave my hand in a dismissive motion. "Not exactly. I'm just kind of camping in my van temporarily. You know, until my mom gets back."

"You mean *if* she gets back?"

I shrug and take another sip.

"I'd ask you to come live with me, but Leon just moved in."

"I know. And really, I'll be okay. I'll probably have enough money to rent a room or an apartment by the end of the month." I pause. "Just *please* don't tell anyone about this. I can't risk my job. *Okay?*"

"Sure. You can trust me, Adele."

"And I'll bring your dress in tomorrow."

She just shakes her head. "I still can't believe you had such a lousy night. Some fairy godmother I am."

I force a smile. "Hey, you tried."

"And I take it back, Adele. You don't have to help Bess tonight."

I get up and chuck my empty can into the recycle bin. "No, I think I could use Bess tonight. It'll be comforting to spend time with someone who's worse off than I am."

Genevieve sighs. "Well, that's probably true."

"And if you want, I'll get Mrs. Ashburn ready for bed afterward."

She chuckles. "What are you? A masochist? Some kind of glutton for punishment?"

"I actually like Mrs. Ashburn."

She rolls her eyes. "But the old girl talks nonstop and it takes like forever to get her ready for bed."

"I don't mind."

"Well, you have more patience than me."

It takes all of my patience to try to get Bess to take in some food. And unless she's absorbing drips of applesauce through her chin, I'm pretty sure it's hopeless. I think she wants to die. And according to head nurse Ellen, Bess made a living will that clearly states she is not to have any artificial means of life support.

I glance over at Bess's silent roommate, an unconscious head-injury victim named Clara. She is hooked up to all kinds of machines that burr and buzz and keep her alive.

"That means no feeding tube," Ellen explained. "So unless you get some food into her, she will probably be gone before long."

I smooth Bess's stringy gray hair away from her forehead. Although her pale eyes have a blank vacant stare, I almost think I see the corners of her shriveled lips curl up ever so slightly. Or maybe it's my imagination. "Oh, Bess, you really do need to eat some food. You're so thin."

I slowly lower the head of her bed like I've been taught, tuck her in, and wish that I knew how to pray. Maybe it's the worn black Bible on her bedside table or the picture of Jesus on her wall or just the fact that poor Bess does not seem long for this world, but I have a feeling she could use a real prayer right now.

Unfortunately, I am of little use in the praying department. It's not that I don't believe in God. It's more that I don't really care. And based on the outcome of my life, I don't think he cares much about me either. Yet I'm certain Bess feels differently. But she is so silent and frozen, lying there with her eyes open but not really here. Unable to speak or communicate, she seems stuck between this world and the next. If there is a next. And it seems the least I could do would be to say a little prayer of comfort.

As I straighten the room a bit, I try to remember the short era when I went to Sunday school with Marcie Moore back in second grade. How was it that teacher prayed? Her words didn't sound memorized, and I know she didn't read the prayers out of a book. Her words had seemed genuine and sincere, and I actually believed that God was listening.

As I wipe down the bathroom sink area, which has only been used by caregivers and nurses, I wonder if Pastor Roland ever makes visits here. I've seen other clergymen around on occasion, but I have a feeling it's the family members who make arrangements for this. So far, I haven't seen any of Bess's family visit. Maybe she, like me, has none.

Finally I decide that although I may not know what I'm doing, it's worth a shot. I go over by Bess's bed, put my hand over hers, and close my eyes. "Dear God, I don't really know you, but I'm sure Bess does. You may have noticed that she has a Bible and a picture of Jesus and everything. Anyway, I'm worried she's not going to be around much longer. And I'm not sure how all this works, but I wish you'd help her during this time. Maybe you already are and I just don't know it. But I think Bess needs a friend, and you seem to be the best candidate. So please help her. And while you're at it . . ."

I pause because I want to say "*if* you're really there," but I'm concerned that Bess might actually be listening, and, if so, I don't want to worry her about God's status. So I continue on a positive note. "Please help Bess . . . and while you're at it, God, maybe you can help me, too." Then I gently squeeze Bess's hand and say, "Amen."

I have no idea whether or not I did that right, but I feel a bit better as I turn off Bess's light and leave the room.

"Did she eat anything?" Ellen asks me as I'm on my way to Mrs. Ashburn's room.

"Not really."

Ellen shakes her head. "I'll call her family in the morning."

"Call her family?"

"To let them know it won't be long. They might want to come say good-bye."

"Oh . . . right." I pause by Mrs. Ashburn's door to see that, as usual, she's not in her room yet. If Mrs. Ashburn had her way, bedtime would be at least an hour later.

"She's still in the dayroom." Ellen frowns. "Good luck."

I find Mrs. Ashburn sitting at a table where a jigsaw puzzle is spread out, and she is intently studying the piece in her hand.

"Good evening, Mrs. Ashburn," I say politely. I know she respects good manners.

She looks up. "Oh, good evening, Adele." She holds a solid blue puzzle piece for me to see. "I'm trying to find the correct place for this."

I frown at the piece. It looks exactly like probably a hundred others. "It looks like sky."

"Unless it's water." She holds up the cover of the jigsaw

puzzle for me to see. "Although the blue in the water has a bit more green in it, I think. Unless it's this part here that's reflecting the sky. In that case, it could be the water."

"Yes, I suppose it could be water." I smile at her. "But it's time to get you ready for bed now."

She frowns at me. "Already? I just started working on this puzzle."

I point to the clock over by the television. "But you can see that it's nearly eight now. You actually should've been in your room a while ago." I move her walker close to her chair and put one hand on her elbow to help her.

"Oh, these silly rules." She shakes her head as she pushes herself to a standing position, then firmly grasps her walker. "No one in the real world goes to bed this early, do they?"

"I wouldn't mind going to bed soon," I admit as I walk by her, waiting with each slow step and wishing she could speed it up a bit. "I'm tired."

"Oh, that's right." She stops walking altogether now, turning to look at me. "You had your big dance last night, Adele. How was it?"

No way do I want to tell her what really happened, but even if I give her a fictionalized version, it will slow her down. "I know, I'll tell you all about it as soon as you're in bed. Okay?"

"Like a bedtime story?" she says eagerly.

"Yes. Like a bedtime story."

Now she begins to move faster, her walker squeaking along as she shuffles behind it, and I begin to fabricate a "happy dance story" in my head. In no time, we are in her room, and as a reward, I tell her about the beginning of the evening (which is actually true) as she allows me to help her get ready for bed. With this distraction technique, we actually make good progress, and it's not quite eight when I've got her tucked in.

"So we got to the hotel," I continue as she leans her head back. "A really impressive one with marble floors and Oriental rugs and fresh flowers and everything. And we go to the dance, which is in this really fancy ballroom. And the music is playing and we dance and dance and dance. The end."

She frowns. "But what happened *at* the dance?"

"Oh, you know." I turn away from her and begin straightening the room. "Just the regular kind of dance things."

"But you gave such lovely details about the rest of your evening, Adele. Why did you stop the story just as it was getting interesting?"

I turn and look at her. It's after eight now and my shift is officially over. I could just say good night and leave, but that seems mean. And yet I really don't want to lie about last night. But at the same time I don't want to tell her the truth.

"Did something bad happen at the dance?"

I shrug. "Let's just say it was a long night, Mrs. Ashburn. And I suppose it was a bit disappointing."

She frowns. "Yes, that's just as I suspected. You know I used to teach in a small high school, and I sometimes chaperoned at those dances. I know what can happen, how hearts can get broken."

I just nod.

"Did your beau hurt you?"

At the kind tone of her voice, a lump grows in my throat.

"You can tell me about it, dear."

I glance over at Mrs. Ashburn's roommate, a quiet woman named Gladys who is already snoozing, and I figure it can't hurt to tell Mrs. Ashburn a bit of the truth. If nothing else, it might play on her sympathies and she won't mind that I have to leave.

"It wasn't exactly my boyfriend," I admit as I go stand by her bed. "It was all of my friends."

Her eyes grow wide. "Oh dear."

"Yes . . . you see, my friends are all very well off. You know what I mean? Their parents are wealthy, and my friends all have their own nice cars and great clothes and no concerns about money. I was trying to fit in with them . . . and it just kind of fell apart when they found out I'm not really one of them."

Mrs. Ashburn looks slightly angry now. "Your friends disowned you for not being rich like them?"

I just nod.

"Well, I think you are better off without friends like that, Adele. They sound like the very worst sort of snobs." She launches into a story about when she was a teenager during the Great Depression and how everyone was poor . . . and how they helped each other . . . and made do . . . and enjoyed the happiest times of their lives.

"It sounds lovely," I say as I tuck her in again.

"What you need, dear, are friends who are like you—hard-working, honest, good."

I smile at her and wish that all her words were true. "Thank you. Now, if you don't mind, I really am tired and my shift is over."

"Yes, yes, you head on home now. Take a hot bath, make yourself a nice cup of tea, go to bed, and get a good night's sleep. And I'm sure your perspective will be much brighter tomorrow."

As I turn off her light, I wish I could follow her recommendation. A hot bath, a cup of tea, a real bed . . . well, that all sounds delightful to me. Instead, I have a cold, damp van, which is starting to smell of dirty laundry, to greet me.

Home sweet home.

On Sunday morning my disposition is as gloomy as the weather. Gray and rainy. It doesn't help that the van is clammy and cold. And smelly. I force myself out of the layers of blankets and bedspreads that serve as my bed, jump into the driver's seat, and, shivering as I start the engine, drive to the Laundromat about half a mile away. At least it's warm in there. And once my things are loaded into washers, I run across the street to get some coffee and a donut. Not exactly a healthy choice, but since I work today, I know I'll have a more nutritious meal later.

While my laundry tumbles, I do homework and charge my phone in a nearby power outlet. And really, it's not a bad setup. In fact, the Laundromat might be a good alternative to the library for doing homework. It's warm, well lit, and has a restroom. Unfortunately, the chairs aren't too comfortable.

By ten thirty, my homework is mostly done, my phone is partially charged, and my clean laundry is folded and piled into a large black trash bag I load into my van. Never mind that my favorite jeans shrunk so much that I might never be able to squeeze into them again. Or that the washer twisted my Gap sweater into something that might fit an orangutan now. At least I have clean clothes to wear.

I drive back to River Woods, park my van, and, since I still have time to spare, check my phone. I know it's probably not realistic, but I'm still hoping my mom will call. Do I think she's going to "rescue" me? Not really. I guess I'd just like to know she's still alive.

I'm surprised that there are three messages from Jayden — two from last night and one from this morning. It's with great apprehension that I listen to the first one.

*"Hey, Adele, where are you? The girls came back from the bathroom saying that you took off. But I can't believe you'd do that to me. I know Bristol said some brutal things, but don't let her get to you. Just call me or come back, okay?"*

I sigh as I wait for the next message, left almost an hour later.

*"Adele, it's me again. I've heard more of what happened in the bathroom, and I'm feeling pretty confused right now. All the girls keep saying that you lied to me, to all of us, and that your mom's not really sick . . . and a bunch of stuff. I'm kind of in shock right now. But the more they tell me, the more I start to believe it's true. Please call me. I want to hear your side of this."*

I swallow hard, unsure that I even want to hear the third message that was left about an hour ago, but before I can shut it down, the message begins.

*"Hi, Adele. It's me again. I really don't know what to think about all this. It would help if you would call. Nothing really makes sense anymore. It's like you aren't really the person I thought you were. Could you please call me and tell me what's up?"*

I look at my little alarm clock. I still have ten minutes before work. Why not just get this over with? So I call Jayden, and I'm actually relieved when it goes to voice mail. "It's me, Jayden," I say in a serious voice. "Some of what you've heard about me is true. Some of it is not. I guess if you want to know the truth, you'll have to listen to my side of the story." I clear my throat. "I'm sorry for taking off like that last night . . . but I just didn't know what else to do. I was pretty sure you wouldn't want to be with me anymore. And really . . . I understand." Then I hang up and take in a deep breath, willing myself not to cry.

Work is a good distraction. And pathetic as it is, seeing poor old Bess (still at death's door) is a good reminder that my life could be worse. From what I've heard, her family has been notified, but so far no one has been here to visit. At the end of the day, I stand by her bedside and make my feeble attempt at a prayer again. I hope it's enough.

I punch the time clock and, feeling tired and hopeless, walk out to my van, where it's still raining. I so don't want to be in that chilly old van again tonight. Even the dayroom in the nursing home seems more inviting, and I wonder if anyone would care if I hung out there to do my homework occasionally. And yet I know that might require some kind of explanation on my part. So far I've been trying to be very careful to protect my employment status. Plus I'm worried that it won't be long before I'm questioned about the presence of Darth Vader in the employee parking lot so much. Although I'm preparing some excuses like "dead battery . . . had to walk home" or "low on gas" or "flat tire." Whatever it takes to get by.

I am always very careful about getting into my van, making sure that no one's around to see. And if someone is around, I simply get in and drive away, then come back later. Although I have a battery-operated reading light I got at Wal-Mart, I try to keep it below the window line. I'm not sure how much these tinted windows conceal, but I'm not taking any chances. I honestly don't know what I'd do if anyone figured this out.

I'm not even that comfortable with the fact that Genevieve knows. Except I think I can trust her. Besides, I know a few little things about her I could hold over her head if I needed to. Not that I'd want to. But self-preservation is first and foremost on my mind these days . . . and nights.

For that reason, I count my money very carefully and actually write out a budget I will try to stick to. No more stupid fake designer shoes. My plan is to live as frugally as possible, to save as much as I can, and hopefully to find a place that's not too far from school, that's cheap to rent—and get into it before the weather turns really cold. Hopefully by mid-November or sooner. That's about a month and two paychecks away. I think it's possible.

In the meantime, I have a secret hiding place where I stash my savings. I use an old plastic flashlight as my "bank." I tightly roll up the bills and slide them into the flashlight's interior, the cavity where the batteries would normally go. Even if anyone saw the flashlight, they probably wouldn't want it since it looks like a piece of junk and doesn't even appear to work anyway. I stash that flashlight deep beneath the passenger seat with some other junk I've put there as a kind of camouflage. I consider getting a bank account, but I'm worried that would require ID and that someone might figure out my age and that I'm living on my own, and I just don't want that kind of trouble.

On Monday morning, I get up early and drive to the high school. In such desperate need of a good shower and cleanup, I almost don't care if anyone sees me scurrying with my backpack into the girls' locker room. Really, what does it matter? But as I'm getting dressed, I remember Jayden. And as unrealistic as it might be, I imagine him being willing to listen to me, to understand my story, and to stand by me. And for that reason, I take the same usual care with my appearance. I want to look like nothing's really changed in my life — like I'm still the same girl Jayden assumed I was. And really, aren't I? Besides that, I know from comments made by Jayden that his parents aren't as well off as the others, and I'm hoping that he, like me, might be tired of trying to keep up. Perhaps he and I can create our own little clique — party of two — leaving the others behind. It seems possible.

But as I go to my morning classes, I don't see Jayden anywhere. I'm not sure if he's avoiding me or just not in school today. And in my classes, I can tell I'm being snubbed by my old "friends." In fact, when I take my old seat in art, Bristol actually stands and goes to sit at a different table. Fine, let her. But I'm a little taken aback when even Lindsey seems to have grown chilly. Still, I decide to ignore it and just focus on my art. My life is about school and survival. That's all.

As I'm on my way to lunch, wondering where I'll sit in the cafeteria, Jayden comes up from behind. "We need to talk," he says quietly.

"Right." I just nod, suspecting the real meaning behind those four little words. But even so, I follow him to a quiet corner and wait.

"I got your message," he says, avoiding my eyes. "And I want to give you a chance to explain yourself. All I ask is that you tell the truth, Adele."

The truth? Actually, it's gotten a little blurry. But I decide this might be my one and only chance, so I will try. "The truth is that my mom ran out on me several weeks ago."

He looks shocked. "Seriously? She just left?"

I nod. "My mom is, well, a little flaky. To be more specific, she's bipolar. And she's done some crazy things before." I sigh. "Although this one pretty much takes the cake."

"So, what about the drug stories going around?"

"Drug stories?" I suddenly remember what Bristol claimed the manager told her. "Oh, well, my mom did have a friend over who smoked some weed. But that's about all there was to that."

Jayden frowns.

"So . . . anyway, I've just been trying to hold my life together as best I can." I shrug. "I'm hoping my mom comes back, but if she doesn't, I plan to get a place of my own and—"

"How can you possibly get a place of your own?"

"I have a job . . . I'm saving my money."

Jayden looks at me like he's looking at a stranger or perhaps an exhibit in the zoo.

"I'm sorry I'm not rich like you and the others," I say defensively. "If being poor is a crime, then I guess I'm guilty." I hold up my hands like I'm ready to have him cuff me. "Go ahead, call the cops, have me locked up."

He almost smiles now. "Just for the record, I'm not rich. And being poor isn't a crime."

I feel a small wave of relief.

"But lying to your friends is wrong."

"Yes." I nod. "And I'm sorry for doing that. But it's like I was trapped."

"So, if you were evicted from your house and your mom's gone . . . where are you living?"

I take in a deep breath, unsure of how much I should really admit, yet I don't want to lie anymore either. "I get to stay where I work."

"Oh . . ." He nods like he gets this, but I can see the question marks in his eyes. And I can tell by the way he steps away, the way he shoves his hands in his pockets and glances over his shoulder—we are done.

"Anyway, it's been fun knowing you, Jayden. I can tell our lives are too different to really work. Besides, I have a lot on my plate. I need to focus on school and my job. So really, thanks for everything." And before he can break up with me, I've broken up with him. And despite the tears burning behind my eyes, I walk away as if I am the winner here. But instead of going to the cafeteria, I go to the library and do my calculus.

I fall into a bit of a slump as the week progresses. Exhausted from work, disrupted sleep patterns, and a hacking cough, I give up on my locker room shower routine, and by the end of the week, I actually wear the same outfit to school two days in a row. My hair is stringy, my clothes are slept in, and I probably stink. But really, who cares? No one talks to me. Even Lindsey in art seems to be afraid of me. Finally at the end of the week, she says something.

"You know there are a lot of rumors going around about you."

I just roll my eyes.

"Don't you even care?"

"People can think what they want. I know what the truth is. Why should I care what they say?"

"So, are you saying the rumors aren't true?"

I look up at her now. Her pencil is poised between her fingers like a long cigarette, and she's studying me closely.

"Why do you even care?"

She kind of shrugs. "Because you seemed like a nice person."

"I *am* a nice person. I just happen to be an *impoverished* nice person. And in some circles, poverty is considered to be a character flaw."

"So, the rumors about drugs aren't true?"

I let out a heavy sigh and just shake my head. "I have *never* used drugs in my life. I don't even drink or smoke cigarettes. I can't stand any of that stuff. And anyone who says differently is a liar."

She nods. "Okay, you don't have to get mad at me. That's kind of what I thought. I just wanted to hear it from you."

"So now you have." I turn my focus back to my drawing, but I feel angry. Why are people repeating that kind of crud about me? What's the point? Don't I have enough grief in my life already? Why does anyone feel the need to add to it? And why did Lindsey feel the need to rub my nose in it? Because that's exactly what her little inquisition felt like to me. I thought she was supposed to be a "Christian" and that Christians were supposed to be kind.

I don't care about any of this. Mean people, nasty rumors, backstabbing "friends," betraying boyfriends . . . I just don't care! The only thing I care about anymore is school and survival.

It's almost Halloween, and although it's my night off from work, I have nothing to do, no place to go, and, it seems, not a friend in the world. I drive my van through town and actually consider going into the mission to see if Pastor Roland is there. But I see the bums lined out on the sidewalk, waiting to be let in for dinner, and I just can't bring myself to do it. I end up at the library where I use the bathroom to clean myself up a bit. And lured by the warmth and the big leather easy chairs, I decide to stick around. But instead of doing homework, I escape into a novel.

Finally it's a bit before closing time, and I go to use the bathroom one more time. While I'm brushing my teeth, someone emerges from one of the stalls. Embarrassed to be caught like this, I tuck my toothbrush back into my pack and stand up straight.

"Someone's into good dental hygiene."

I glance over to see the same girl I saw in this very bathroom once before. I can't recall her name, but I know she goes to my school, and I do remember that Jayden said she was homeless. I flash back to the time I watched her washing in the sink. She did look a bit like a transient then. But her clothes seem clean and nice tonight. She seems a bit more together, which makes me wonder if her luck has changed.

"You're Adele Porter, aren't you?" She washes her hands in the sink.

I wipe a stray bit of toothpaste from the corner of my mouth. "Yes. You go to Stanfield High too, right?"

She nods. "Cybil Henderson."

"Nice to meet you." I make what feels like a strange little smile.

"Lots of rumors going around the school about you this week."

"Really?" For some reason this surprises me. I mean, the way I've been ignored made me assume that I was also forgotten.

"Oh yeah." She dries her hands and turns to look at me. "I think you and me have some things in common."

I take in a deep breath, then slowly release it. "You mean being homeless?"

Her brow creases slightly. "Yeah . . . that too."

"So, you really are homeless?" Suddenly I'm remembering Mrs. Ashburn's advice to me about getting friends who, like me, know how it feels to be poor.

"Pretty much so."

"So, what do you do? I mean, where do you stay?"

Cybil shrugs. "Here and there."

"On the streets?"

She kind of laughs. "Not on a cold night like this."

"So, where then?"

"I have a few friends. I do some couch surfing."

"Oh."

"How about you?" She peers closely at me like she's really curious. "Who are your friends now that the rich witch girls have dumped you?"

I consider this. I might be homeless, but I still have my pride. I'm not about to admit I don't have friends. "I have friends I hang with at work," I say with mock confidence.

"You have a job?"

"I do. And I'm saving up enough to get a place of my own too."

She actually seems impressed by this. "Cool."

Now I feel my guard dropping a little. "But it's still kind of lonely."

She nods. "I know."

The door opens and a librarian sticks her head in the bathroom. "Closing time, ladies."

"Yeah, yeah," Cybil says. "We're outta here."

Soon Cybil and I are outside, and I'm not really sure what to say. "It was cool meeting you," I tell her as we go down the stairs.

"Yeah. You too."

"So, where do you go from here?" I ask out of pure curiosity.

She jerks her thumb over her shoulder. "I have a friend with an apartment over on Third Avenue. He'll let me crash there tonight."

"Do you need a ride?"

She looks shocked. "Seriously? Do you have a car?"

"Yeah." I point to the black van and the only vehicle left in the patron section of the parking lot.

"Cool." She nods eagerly. "Sure, I'd love a ride."

"It's kind of an ugly van," I admit as we get inside. "I call it Darth Vader."

She laughs. "Fitting name." She looks into the back. "Do you live here?"

"Pretty much."

"Very cool!"

"And kind of cold, too," I confess as I start the engine. "But I bundle up and I have a lot of bedding, so it's not too bad. Hopefully it won't be for too much longer."

She directs me to a run-down apartment complex, then invites me to come up and meet her friend. Curious as to what kind of place this might be and what the rent would run, I accept her offer. But when I see the dump of an apartment and several seedy-looking older guys sitting around drinking, I decide to cut my visit short.

"Don't go yet," a guy named Tony tells me. "You just got here."

"I know." I force a smile. "But I have to work in the morning."

"A working girl, eh?" says a guy who looks to be around thirty.

"Come on," urges Tony. "Stick around and have a beer."

"Thanks anyway. But I really need to go. Maybe another time."

"Okay." He nods like I just made a date with him. "I'm holding you to that!"

I tell Cybil good-bye then, relieved to get away, and hurry back to the van. Maybe Cybil's friends are okay. Or maybe they're not. I really don't want to find out. For the most part they remind me of a younger version of some of the guys my mom hooked up with over the years. Losers.

Cybil actually seems to have more going for her than those dudes in the cruddy apartment. In fact, it makes me wonder why she'd settle for that. Except that she is homeless. And, like me, her options are limited.

## CHAPTER 15

Halloween isn't until Friday, but it seems that I picked the one night the library is celebrating to do my homework here. Fortunately, story hour (complete with a witch) is over, and the place quiets back down into what I expect a library to be. I'm just settling back into my history when Cybil joins me.

"Hey." She plops down in an easy chair across from me. "How's it going?"

"Okay." I set my book down. "How about you?"

"I've had better days."

"Meaning?"

She rubs her stomach. "I'm starving."

Now this statement coming from some people is just an exaggeration. But from a homeless person, well, it gets my attention. And since I worked today, I've had plenty to eat. So naturally, I feel bad for her. "I can loan you a couple of bucks," I offer, knowing full well this will crunch my lunch budget tomorrow.

She brightens. "Cool." Then her smile fades. "Except I don't know when I can pay you back."

I wave my hand. "It's okay."

"I was going to do some panhandling at the grocery store down the street, but a cop came along and I zipped over here."

"Can you get arrested for panhandling?"

"It's illegal in our town."

"Oh . . ." I nod as I dig a couple bucks and some loose change from my purse. "Good to know."

"Yeah. The cops don't do much besides take your information—and I always lie about where I live. I give them my aunt's old address, and they don't seem to know the difference since it's a rental house anyway. Mostly they just try to scare you off the streets."

I hand her the cash. "How many times have you been picked up for panhandling anyway?"

"Just a couple. I know to be more careful now." She tucks the money into her coat pocket. "Thanks."

"So, where are you staying tonight?"

She shrugs. "I don't know."

I want to question her about her low-life guy friends in the sleazy apartment, but it's not really my business. Still, I'd like to warn her to be careful. "How old are you anyway?"

"Almost sixteen."

I try not to look shocked. "So . . . what year are you in school?"

"Sophomore."

"Oh . . ."

"Yeah, I know what you're thinking."

"What?"

"How am I going to do it? Make it through almost three years of high school while living on the streets."

"Hey, I'm pretty concerned about just making it through the next seven months so I can graduate and get out of this town."

"Yeah, well, maybe I won't graduate."

"You'd drop out?"

"I could get my GED," Cybil says.

"And then what?"

"A job . . . or get married."

"But you're so young."

"Age is just a number, Adele."

"I know . . ." And for no explainable or rational reason, I start to feel almost big sisterly toward Cybil just now. "But quitting high school . . . to work or to get married . . . it just doesn't seem like a good plan."

She looks exasperated. "It's not like I planned all this."

"I know." I nod. "Neither did I. My mom just took off, and I'm trying to make the best of it."

"Your mom ditched you, too?"

"Is that what happened to you?"

"Kind of." She scowls. "First my mom took off and I ended up with my grandma. That was back when I was just starting middle school. But when I broke a few of Granny's silly little rules, she got fed up and dumped me on my aunt. That was okay for a while, but last summer, my aunt went back to her ex and told me to go home to Granny." She shakes her head. "No way was I doing that."

"But you could, if you wanted?"

She rolls her eyes. "Yeah, and I could be locked up in juvy too. Same difference."

"Have you ever been in foster care?" I ask quietly.

She nods. "When my mom ditched me with the neighbors, supposedly for the weekend, but she never came back. They called Children's Services and I ended up in the foster-care home from hell."

I actually laugh. "Hey, I was in that one too."

Cybil's eyes get wide. "Were you sexually abused?"

I shake my head. "No . . . I mean . . . you know, almost. How about you?"

She just nods.

"Sorry."

She shrugs. "Hey, at least it got me out of there when I reported it to my social worker. That's when I got sent to Granny's house. Unfortunately, Granny never liked kids. Guess that's what went wrong with my mom and my aunt."

We continue to talk, and I'm surprised at how many similarities there are to our stories. Maybe that's how it is for a lot of kids. I guess I never really thought about it much, or I assumed I was all alone in this madness.

"Sometimes I feel like I'm just this worthless piece of garbage," Cybil says sadly, "like no one wanted me in the first place and no one wants me now. People get uncomfortable when they see me coming; they look the other way."

"I know what you mean. That's how I've been feeling lately." Admitting this isn't easy. "It's like everyone is treating me like a pariah."

"What's that?"

"Pariah?" I shrug. "You know . . . something to be avoided. An outcast."

"You really are smart, aren't you?"

I attempt a laugh. "I wasn't too smart in my choice of friends. That's obvious by the way they're treating me now."

"But that's how you used to treat me."

"What?"

"Remember the first time you saw me in the bathroom and you stepped away from me like you thought I was contagious? Like you were worried you might catch something from me?"

"Sorry."

"Hey, I am used to it." She pushes a strand of dishwater blond hair behind an ear. "But look, you're in the same boat now."

I nod. "It's weird. I got a feeling that day, or maybe it was a premonition, but it's like I knew deep inside of me that I wasn't much different than you. But I was trying to pretend . . ."

"Don't you think that's what everyone does . . . just tries to pretend? Like the snooty kids you used to hang with. I mean, think about it, if their parents ditched them, they'd be in the same place we are right now. How would they feel then?"

"Good point." I smile at her. "You know, Cybil, you seem like an intelligent person. I don't know why you'd even consider dropping out of school."

"Other than the fact I might have no choice."

"Of course you have a choice." I pause to think. "What if you got a part-time job?"

She frowns. "Yeah right. What would be the point?"

"The point would be that if you had some income, you and I could get an apartment together—we wouldn't be homeless anymore."

"Really?" Her whole face lights up now. "You'd consider doing that with me?"

"Why not? Like you said, we're in the same boat. Why not help each other row for the shore?"

Now her smile fades. "But who would hire me?"

"Lots of people." I tell her about my unusual employment history, which began when I was a lot younger than her. I explain how she can get a food handlers card and make a résumé and all sorts of things. "I could even help you with your résumé, and we could print it out right here on one of the library computers."

"That would be cool. When do we start?"

I glance at the big clock over the reception desk. "Not tonight; it's almost closing time." I start to put my books back into my bag.

"Yeah. Anyway, I am seriously starving."

"Want me to give you a lift?"

She shrugs. "Sure, but I don't even know where I'm going. I mean, besides Burger King for their one-buck specials."

As we go outside and down the library steps, I can tell that it's even colder now than when I got off work. "So, you really don't know where you're staying tonight?" I ask once we're inside the van.

"I could crash at Tony's . . ." I hear the reservation in her voice.

"No offense, Cybil, but that didn't seem like such a great place." I stop for the traffic light and hope I'm not overstepping any boundaries.

"Maybe not to you, since you have your warm, dry van to stay in, but trust me, it beats sleeping under a bridge."

I consider pointing out that while Darth Vader might be dry, it's certainly not warm—but decide not to. After all, isn't this all kind of relative? Now we ride in silence to Burger King. But when Cybil gets out, she slams the door so hard the van rocks. And okay, I'm pretty sure I've offended her. For all I know, she might not even come back or speak to me again. And why should that bother me? Don't I have enough problems of my own without going out looking for more?

And yet I feel bad. It has been interesting getting to know this girl . . . almost like a friendship. Still, what's the point? Why not just drive away and forget it? I suppose I'm lonely . . . or maybe just desperate. But for whatever reason, when I see Cybil emerging from Burger King with a take-out bag in hand,

I decide to make up for my bad manners. I open the window and, stifling a cough, call her back over to the van.

"Look"—I give an awkward smile—"maybe you could try spending the night in the van for one night."

"Seriously?"

I nod, coughing as I wave her around to the passenger side. "Hurry, get in."

"Thanks!" She runs around to the other side and hops in.

"Yeah. We'll see how it goes. Maybe we'll figure out that we don't get along and we should never be roommates." I cough as I start up the engine.

"You should take something for that cough," she tells me as I pull into traffic.

"Oh, it comes and goes." As I head toward the nursing home, I explain about my job, how I park in the River Woods parking lot, but how we must be very careful not to be seen.

"No problem," she says with a mouthful of food. "I'm used to keeping a low profile. And I used the Burger King restroom, so I'm good for the night."

Naturally the van is much more crowded with Cybil, but after I do some rearranging, I have to admit it's comforting having company. And she doesn't complain. Now I'm really thankful that I took all the bedding from the condo. We need it. After we're in our makeshift bed, we actually talk for a while, but eventually she drifts off to sleep and I'm left lying there feeling a whole bunch of mixed emotions.

On one hand, it feels good to help someone in need . . . on the other hand, I wish someone would help me. Then I remember what my mom used to say about karma: "What goes 'round comes 'round . . . be good to others and others will be good to you." And while that makes sense on some levels, it hasn't exactly been my personal experience. I mean, I try to be good to everyone, yet here I am homeless. Meanwhile my mom — who's been more of a taker than a giver — for all I know she is out there living the good life somewhere. Or not. Anyway, life seems more like a coin toss than karma to me.

I actually feel a tiny bit more optimistic the next morning. Cybil seems genuinely appreciative of my hospitality, and on our way to school, she talks seriously about finding a job and the prospects of us sharing an apartment.

"I'm a good cook," she says. "And I know how to keep house too. My grandma saw to that. So if I tried, I think I could be a pretty good roommate."

"I'll start looking for apartments after the first," I tell her. "If you got a job right away, we might be able to get into something before Thanksgiving."

"Cool." She nods happily as we get out of the van.

As we walk toward school, I explain how I have to leave after seventh period to have time to change my clothes and make it to work on time. "But if you want a ride, just meet me out here."

"Sounds good to me."

"And I'll run inside the nursing home to find an old Classifieds section of the newspaper to bring back to you. And you can start looking for jobs and working on that résumé. Okay?"

"Sure."

I'm surprised at how good it feels to be helping someone. It's like my problems suddenly seem smaller and I actually feel nearly normal until I see Bristol giving me that look in art class. I'm not even sure how someone can look down her nose at someone who is the same height, but Bristol has this expression down pat. Usually I ignore her, but honestly I just wish she'd get over it.

Instead of saying something snide, like I'm tempted to do, I go directly to my table and get to work sketching a tree onto my watercolor paper. Then to my surprise, Lindsey, who has been fairly tight lipped since my "fall from friends," actually speaks to me. At first I think I imagined it, but then she says something else.

"That tree is turning out pretty good."

"Thanks." I still don't look up, keeping my eyes on my paper. And for a while we both work quietly. She's beyond the sketching stage now, and I can hear her watercolor brush dipping into the jar of water and tap-tap-tapping against the glass.

"I noticed you talking with Cybil Henderson at the library last night." Lindsey's voice is low, like she wants to keep this private. "Do you think that's wise?"

I frown up at her. *"Wise?"*

"Remember what we talked about last week?"

"Huh?"

"You told me you weren't into drugs."

"Yeah." I cock my head to one side, just studying her, trying to figure out what her game is.

"Well, you might not want to hang with someone like Cybil Henderson then."

Okay, this just seriously irks me. Lindsey, the perfect little librarian's helper, the perfect little Christian, getting ready to take her perfect little European vacation—and she's telling me to ditch my one and only friend? Little Miss Perfect wants me to dump a poor homeless girl who's already been ditched by (1) her mom, (2) her grandmother, and (3) her aunt. What is wrong with this picture?

"I'm just saying that you need to be careful about your friends," Lindsey continues, like she's some kind of expert in this area, or maybe she thinks she's a social worker.

"You know, I think I've learned a thing or two about friends recently," I say in a tone that's sharper than I intended.

Lindsey nods. "But not all lessons have to be learned the hard way."

I grip my pencil so tightly that I'm surprised it doesn't snap.

"I'm just trying to help you, Adele." She makes an apologetic smile.

"Help *me*?" I'm suppressing the urge to scream right now. "You really want to help me?"

She shrugs. "I just think you could be more selective in choosing your friends."

I take in a slow, deep breath, mentally counting to ten. Then I look evenly at her. "It's weird, Lindsey. I haven't noticed that you have any friends. In fact, you seem like a bit of a loner to me. Isn't it ironic that you're giving me advice on friends?"

I can tell I got her with that zapper. Without saying a word, she dips her brush in the water and returns to her painting. But I am still fuming inside. I press my pencil to the paper so firmly that the lead snaps. And I can relate to that. I feel like I'm about to snap too. Seriously, what is wrong with people?

ybil and I seem to be getting along okay, and by the end of the week, we've actually made progress on her résumé and lined up some possible places for her to apply. I've been coaching her on how to do an interview, and we're planning an outfit for her to wear. I actually feel fairly positive about the prospects.

"We're invited to a Halloween party tonight," Cybil tells me on Friday as I'm driving us home from school. "You have the night off, right?"

"What party?" I ask with a mix of suspicion and hopefulness. On one hand, it would be cool to go to a real Halloween party . . . on the other, it could be a skanky party.

"A Halloween party," she says like I wasn't listening.

"Who's hosting the party?"

She laughs. "Hosting?"

"You know what I mean. Where's the party?"

"At Tony's."

Okay, that's more than enough information for me. "Thanks, but no thanks."

"Why not?"

"Because I get a bad feeling about those guys."

"Oh, Adele. Why are you so judgmental? They're nice guys. And it'll be fun."

"Fun?" I glance at her. "Tell me, how do you describe fun?"

"You know . . . some laughs, some friends, some drinks."

"I can go with the laughs and friends—I mean, if they're real friends—but I'll pass on the drinks."

"Fine, you can pass. But you can at least come to the party."

"I don't want to go, Cybil."

"Oh, Adele!" She folds her arms across her front and slumps down in the passenger seat like she's about four years old.

"Sorry, Cybil. I just don't want to. And I don't think you should go either." I'm pulling into the River Woods parking lot now. This time I park in the guest section.

She jerks around and stares at me. "Are you telling me what I can or cannot do now?"

I turn off the ignition and sigh. "I'm just saying I think it's a mistake to keep hanging with people like Tony and those other guys."

"You *are* telling me what to do!" Her voice is getting shrill.

"I'm trying to be a friend to you, Cybil. And I'm older and I just don't think you should go. Maybe we can do something else and—"

"What are you, Adele, *my mother*?"

Now for some reason this just totally irks me. "Look," I say in a sharp voice, "I'm trying to help you, but if you're going to act like an idiot . . ."—I hold up my hands like I'm done—"then don't come running back to me when you get in trouble."

"So that's it?" She's glaring at me. "You'll be my friend as long as I do what you want me to do? If you can control me, you'll help me?"

"I don't want to control—"

"You're just like my grandma, Adele. An old stick-in-the-mud."

"Fine," I snap at her. "At least I know how you feel."

"Fine!"

Then we both sit there in silence, and I'm hoping her common sense will kick in and she'll realize what a fool she's being to even consider going back to those jerk guys when I'm trying to offer her a way to get off the streets.

"Tell me something, Cybil."

She just makes a harrumph sound, but I decide to continue. "What exactly goes on in Tony's apartment?"

"What do you mean?"

"Well, I know there's alcohol there."

"Yeah, so?"

"And I assume there might be drugs, too."

She doesn't say anything, which I take as a confirmation.

"And I saw the way the guys were looking at us; I heard what they said, so I assume there's an expectation of sex."

Still, she's silent.

"And I'm sorry, but I have higher standards than that."

"That's your choice," she says in a pouty tone.

"You're right. It is. But this is my van, and if you're going to live with me, it has to be your choice too." I'm trying to keep my voice calm and nonconfrontational now, something I learned from years of "getting along" with my mom.

"What right do you have to impose your morality on me?" she shoots back at me. "You don't own me, Adele. And you never will. If I want to go party with my friends, you are not going to stop me!"

I just nod as a lump wedges itself into my throat. This all feels so familiar—like a flashback to a past conversation with my mom.

"So that's it then?" She climbs into the back of the van and starts stuffing her things into her backpack. "You're through with me just because I want to go to a stupid Halloween party?" Now she's swearing and crashing about, and I'm worried that she's really losing it. "You're just like the rest of my family. You act like you care about me, and then you toss me out like the trash. Well, I don't know why I'm even surprised by that. I never should've trusted you in the first place."

"Excuse me for caring about you," I say with a sarcastic edge. "I'm sorry I don't want to see you ruining—"

She interrupts me with a few more choice expletives before she slides open the back door with a bang, then leaps out of the van. Pausing in the parking lot, she gives me the middle-finger salute, then throws a strap of her backpack over her shoulder and stomps away, leaving the door wide open as a rush of cold air whooshes in.

I cough as I hurry to slide the door shut. Then I climb into the back, wrap myself up in my old quilt, and just sit there shivering. What could I have done differently? Why did I ever try in the first place? Seriously, who has room for all this drama? Certainly not me.

Now I remember that Ms. Michaels said since October is a long month, we could pick up our checks today instead of tomorrow. So I hurry into River Woods and find my envelope in my time-card slot, remove it, and leave. I go to the check-cashing place, where they charge me ten bucks just to cash my check. But feeling good to have the money in my hand, I drive back to River Woods and settle in for the night. Maybe a good night's rest will help to get rid of this cough I'm having a hard time shaking.

But the next morning I wake up coughing and shivering.

And there's frost on the windows of the van—this is not good. Still wrapped in my layers of blankets, I squirm over to where my flashlight bank is hidden. I added my latest earnings to it last night but never took the time to figure out the total. So I empty it all out now, and organizing the bills, I count. As badly as I'd like to save up enough to rent an apartment by the month, this cold weather makes me think it might be time to look into another form of accommodations. Maybe even one of those somewhat sleazy motels downtown, the kind that rent rooms by the week. I've done the math and that ends up costing more in the long run, but I'm not sure I have a choice anymore. Be frugal and freeze to death, or tap my budget and survive? This is about survival.

Then the sun comes out, warming the van a bit, and as I get ready for work, I think perhaps I'm giving up too easily. Either I can bundle up better and hold out a couple more weeks, or maybe I can make a deal with a landlord, pay two months' rent, and promise to pay the cleaning deposit by the end of November. I do the math in my head, and it will make my budget tight but it seems possible.

After punching in at work, I put my time card back into its slot and notice that Genevieve's time card is missing. I don't think too much of this, but a few minutes later when I'm in the dining room, picking up a sweater Mr. Lupinksi left behind, I overhear Ellen talking to Mary in the kitchen.

"You were right," she tells Mary. "Genevieve had been stealing. Ms. Michaels has already called her and informed her of her termination."

"I told you," Mary says victoriously. "I have a good sense about these things."

"Yes, and we appreciate it."

"If I wasn't such a good chef, I might go into the security business." Mary laughs like this is really funny.

With sweater in hand, I scurry away. I'm not sure which is more shocking: that Genevieve has been fired, or that she's been stealing from River Woods. Then as I help Mr. Lupinski into his old worn cardigan, I wonder if Genevieve really did steal anything or if she's been falsely accused. It's no secret that she and Mary do not get along. But then no one really gets along with Mary. And if Genevieve actually did steal something, how exactly did Mary find out?

I'm aware there are video cams placed here and there, both for security and to document any "alleged mistreatment of residents." I also know there's one out in the parking lot. I make sure to park just outside of its scope. Still, I can't help but be concerned that Mary might be watching me as well. Maybe it's time to park my van elsewhere during the night.

I've just gotten Mr. Lupinski settled back into his room and am emerging into the hallway, trying to muffle my cough into my sleeve, when Ms. Michaels approaches me. "I'd like to talk to you, Adele."

I just nod, force a little smile, and follow her to her office. And maybe I'm paranoid, but I feel certain that Mary has informed on me as well. I am about to get the ax.

"You probably heard about Genevieve by now," she says somberly.

"Not exactly."

So she tells me how things have been missing from the kitchen and how Mary rigged up a hidden video cam that caught Genevieve red-handed.

"Oh no." I just shake my head. "I had no idea."

"Naturally, I had to let her go."

"Naturally." I wait.

"Well, I know you were good friends with Genevieve, so I felt you should know."

"I appreciate that." I nod.

"And that means there will be a bit more work for you until I can hire another nurse's aide. But hopefully I'll get that taken care of by Monday."

"That's okay; I like being busy."

She smiles. "Yes, it hasn't escaped my notice that you're a hard worker."

Now I feel a cough coming. I turn and cough into the elbow of my sleeve. "Excuse me."

"Are you taking anything for that?"

"I've been meaning to get something."

"Well, go ask Ellen to give you something for it. We can't have you coughing on the residents."

"No, I try not to cough around them. And I wash my hands all the time too."

She smiles again. "Yes, I know you do."

So I go find Ellen, explaining what Ms. Michaels said, and she gives me a small sample bottle of cough medicine. I take the prescribed dose and put the remainder in my backpack to use later.

Genevieve's absence does make me busier, but it also makes the time pass more quickly. And before I know it, my shift is over. I clock out and head for my van, which I have decided to park someplace else for the night. I'm actually considering going back to the visitor area of the condos. Hopefully no one will notice or care. Then tomorrow I will come up with a different plan.

But when I get to the parking lot, I notice what appears

to be broken ice along the passenger side of the van. But upon closer inspection, I see that it's actually broken glass. The passenger-side window has been broken out. I jerk open the door to find that my van has been broken into. Stuff is strewn all over the place, and although it's hard to tell at first glance, it seems like a number of things are missing.

I turn on the dome light and, with a pounding heart, go through my belongings, sorting them, folding them, methodically putting them away. As I work, I realize that two pairs of jeans, a sweater, some T-shirts, my favorite boots, some sweats, some bedding, my alarm clock, and much more are gone. And as much as I hate to think this, I know deep inside of me that Cybil is the culprit. Who else would know what was in my van? And only a girl would want my clothes. It has to be her.

And then, like a punch to my gut, I remember my flashlight. Surely she didn't take that too. Then I remind myself as much as I trusted Cybil, I never once told her where I stashed my savings. In fact, I think she assumed I had a bank account, which was fine by me.

I hit the floor behind the passenger seat and claw around beneath it, digging out the other bits of junk I stashed there as camouflage. But I cannot feel the flashlight anywhere. It's not there. Then I sit up and try to think. Did I put it someplace else and forget?

Suddenly I remember how I counted out my money this morning, trying to decide if I had enough to get an apartment yet. I must've forgotten to replace it beneath the seat. Still, why would Cybil take an old flashlight? How could she have known what was inside it? Like a crazy person, I tear apart what I've just organized in my van, throwing the blankets and the few clothes I have left onto the seats as I search in vain for the missing flashlight.

Finally I realize it's no use. I collapse in a fit of coughing and tears. It is not here! Every dollar I worked so hard to earn and save is gone—just like that, it is gone. Not only that, but my van is useless as a haven now. It's as cold inside as it is outside. There is no way I can survive like this. Because my shift ended at eight, I know it must be well past nine by now, and I have to work again tomorrow. Not that it makes any difference now. Really, what am I working for? What am I living for?

I bundle up as well as I can, layering on what few shabby clothes I have left, wrapping myself in blankets, and then I finish off the rest of the cough medicine. I don't even care if it's an overdose. Really, it would be just fine if I never woke up. Dying cannot possibly be worse than living . . . not like this.

To my surprise and disappointment, I am still here in the morning. I did not die during the night. At least I don't think I died. I sit up and stare out the fogged window as a dark gray hearse pulls into the parking lot. Creeping along as if, like me, it does not want to be observed. As I watch the hearse coming closer, I can almost make myself believe it's here for me . . . that I did die in the night and I'm simply imagining I'm alive. But then it slowly backs up to the rear entrance of River Woods, and I realize that one of the residents must've passed on during the night. The hearse must be here for Bess.

As part of my usual routine, I lingered by her bedside last night. I held her hand and mumbled my feeble attempt of a prayer. But before I left, I did notice that her eyes were closed and her expression was no longer that of a frightened old woman balancing on the edge of life. In fact, her facial muscles seemed relaxed, as if she was at peace. At least she is in a better place. I try not to be envious. I'm not sure I can even imagine what that would be like — a better place . . . peace — it's beyond my grasp.

Then realizing that someone from River Woods might come out the back door to speak to the hearse driver and subsequently notice my vandalized van still parked here, I decide to make a quick getaway. Before long, I'm sitting in the nearest coffee shop, where I plan to thaw out until it's time for my shift. But my mind feels blurry and slow, like I can't even run my thoughts in a straight line.

"You look like you've lost your best friend," the waitress tells me as she refills my cup.

I just nod. "Yeah . . . I kind of did."

"I'm sorry." She gives me a sad smile. "But take it from me, dearie, it's always darkest before the dawn."

"Thanks. I'll try to keep that in mind."

I feel like a zombie as I go through the paces at River Woods. I know I should be concerned about putting my job in jeopardy, but I really don't care anymore. And as I'm punching my time card at the end of my shift, I know I should be making a plan to head to the library or somewhere else warm to do my homework. But it's like something in me is broken now . . . like I don't even care about school anymore. Really, what difference does it make how hard I try to make my life work? It always goes wrong in the end.

On my way out, I pass by Bess's old room. Maybe it's habit or maybe I miss her, but I feel drawn into the room. It's quiet as usual, and her silent roommate is still hooked up to various forms of life support. I stand there staring at Clara's pale face, so oblivious to this world. Her family members come and go, workers see to her needs, and yet she is completely unaware. I wonder at this irony—a woman who may not even want to be alive is being kept and cared for (at an expense I cannot even comprehend), and yet I am broke and homeless and left to my own sad devices to survive. How is that fair?

I go and stand by Bess's empty bed, placing my hand on the pillow. The bedding has been changed, and a new resident will probably be here soon. If Bess were still alive, I would probably be praying right now. With her gone, I cannot utter a word. Instead I remove my shoes and climb into her bed. I know it's pathetic and creepy, not to mention foolish because this could cost me my job. But I'm so worn out, so defeated . . . I just don't care anymore. If someone wants to fire me for sleeping in a dead woman's bed, let them. Just bring it.

When I wake it's to the quiet murmur of voices, and although my eyes are still closed, I sense that it's lights-out. At first I can't remember where I am. All I know is I was having a lovely dream — walking barefoot in a place where it was warm and sunny and bright. Heaven perhaps? Without moving and with my eyes still shut, I strain my ears to understand the whispered words, to process what they're saying.

"What is she doing in here?" It sounds like Ellen.

"I don't know, but I think she's been here all night."

"Ugh, I wonder how she can stand to sleep in a bed that someone just died in." This comes from a man's voice.

"Oh, it's just a bed, silly," Ellen says.

"Should we wake her?"

"Ms. Michaels will have to hear about this." This is followed by what I imagine to be Ellen's footsteps walking away, off to find the boss. I wait a few more seconds, wishing none of this was really happening. Then I open my eyes and sit up to see a night orderly named Neal and a nurse's aide I don't really know. They are both staring at me with slightly stunned expressions.

Without saying a word, I climb out of bed, slip on my shoes, and leave.

"Hey wait," the nurse's aide calls. "I think Ellen wants to talk to you."

Now I'm faced with a choice. I'm pretty sure my job here is

about to be terminated anyway, so I might as well keep going. But I've never been the kind to just walk out on a job. I guess I'm not ready to start now. So I head toward the office area and soon am sitting in front of Ellen. Without waiting for her to question me, I simply pour out my sad little tale. I don't give all the details. But I do give enough to ensure that I will be jobless when I leave the room. All the "less" words seem to describe my status now — jobless, homeless, penniless, hopeless, friendless. All I need to add to the list is lifeless. Then it would be complete.

"Please tell Ms. Michaels I'm sorry for being such a disappointment," I say as I stand. "But I just can't do this anymore." Then I walk out. And this time I just keep going.

I get in the van and drive away from River Woods. I have no idea where I'm going. And I don't care. I just drive away. I know the gas tank is nearly empty. I know I have less than ten dollars in my backpack. I know the cold air and rain are rushing in through my broken window. And after a while, I know that I'm having difficulty seeing the lines on the road. I turn my wipers to high speed, but it doesn't get better. That's when I realize my vision is blurred by tears streaming down. So I pull into a 7-Eleven and turn off the engine, lean my head into the steering wheel, and just cry.

I've reached the end . . . I cannot go on. I don't want to. I just want all of this to end. If someone gave me a magic button that would erase me from the face of the earth right now, I would be relieved to push it.

Finally I have no more tears left to cry. I pick up a slightly used Burger King napkin from the floor of the van, blow my nose on it, and just look around. I have no idea what to do next. Where to go? What does it matter? Then I notice a wrinkled business card sitting on my dashboard. I pick it up and stare at the words. They look foreign and unreal to me. *Mercy and Grace Community Church.* But I remember Pastor Roland at the mission; he seemed real. And I remember what he said—how I could ask him and his church for help. I wonder if he really meant it.

With nothing to lose, and since the address of the church doesn't look far from this 7-Eleven, I decide to drive over and check it out. Before long, I'm driving past a small white church, and I'm surprised that the parking lot in back is nearly filled with cars, but then I remember it's Sunday. So I park my van, and feeling almost like a sleepwalker or maybe an alien, I get out of the van and go directly into the church.

Before the door barely closes behind me, I'm tempted to turn and flee, but the warmth lures me in. I go into what seems like an old-fashioned sanctuary—the kind you see in an old movie, complete with wooden pews, stained-glass windows, and several dozen old people with open books in their hands, singing slightly off tune but with enthusiasm.

I sit in the back as they continue singing, and while the music is completely unfamiliar, it's kind of soothing. But I notice some uncomfortable glances tossed in my direction. Not obvious, but I know people are looking at me . . . then looking away again. Almost as if I'm not really here. That's when I notice the people in here are nicely dressed—probably wearing their "Sunday best." Men have on suits and ties. The women look nice too. Everyone looks neat and clean. I look down at my stained jacket and wrinkled pants. I must look like a bum to them. Oh, that's right, I am a bum.

Even so, I continue sitting there and listen as a man, not Pastor Roland, reads from what I can only assume is a Bible. The words sound like another language and go right over my head.

And then Pastor Roland steps up to the wooden podium and begins to talk. I try to take in his words, but quite honestly, I feel confused by them. He's speaking about goodness and kindness and generosity . . . and how love changes the world. But all I can think of is — *what love?* Where is it? Why have I never been on the receiving end of all this fairy-tale generosity and love? Does it even exist? I feel like I'm ravenous and starving, watching one of those food channels where everything looks so delicious I can almost smell it. And although I might be salivating, there is no real food here — not for me anyway. It's all an illusion, a mean trick.

And so as quietly as I came in, I slip back out again. But as I drive away from the little white church, I feel confused and betrayed. Why did Pastor Roland think that I would find what I needed there? How can those people help me? It felt as if they couldn't even see me, didn't want to see me. I'm sure my presence made them uncomfortable.

I drive around some more, trying to think, but my thoughts are like tennis shoes tumbling in a dryer, rattling and thumping, disconnected and random. Nothing makes sense. And then just as I'm accelerating after a red stoplight, nothing happens. My foot presses the gas, but the van is not moving. The engine is dead. I am out of gas.

Horns are honking behind me now, and I don't know what to do. Feeling desperate, I climb into the back of the van, quickly gather up everything I can stuff into my backpack or carry, then exit through the sliding side door. I hear horns beeping and people yelling unkind remarks and the sounds of engines as drivers maneuver their cars around the big black barricade formerly known as Darth Vader. But I don't look back as I hurry away with my belongings in my arms. I have no idea what will happen to the van. Why should I care?

By the time I stop walking, I'm out of breath and slightly disoriented. Mostly I just wanted to get away, but now I realize that I'm in the center of town, not far from the swanky hotel that hosted the homecoming dance. That night feels like another lifetime now. I can feel people's curious glances as I walk with my backpack on my back and my arms filled with my other belongings. I feel them stepping aside just slightly, avoiding me like they're worried I might contaminate them or perhaps that I'm going to pester them for money.

I remember what Cybil said about panhandling. Is this one of the areas she frequented? I must admit that the idea of picking up a few bucks is tempting, and the threat of arrest isn't even terribly disturbing now. Really, would jail be so bad? A bed, warmth, food—why would I complain? I also remember how Cybil said there were numerous ways of getting money. I didn't press her for details, but I'm fairly certain she traded her body for money upon occasion.

Just thinking of Cybil makes me angry. Why did I ever let her into my life? Look where it got me! But as I walk, I realize I don't have the energy to be angry and survive. I must choose. I know I'm on my way to the mission now. I'm not even sure what I expect they can do for me there, but I hope to get a meal, perhaps even a bed. After that, I don't know. But I have a feeling I won't be in school tomorrow.

The following week is all about survival. School is a dim memory now. My focus is on getting food, finding a place to sleep, and keeping my stuff from being stolen. I learned this lesson the hard way my first night at the mission. I stupidly left my backpack under my bed and woke up to discover that my dead cell phone, nearly empty wallet, and several other things were missing. Now I sleep with my backpack cradled in my arms like a baby. I would report this theft to the police, but that might mean I need to divulge my age . . . and risk ending up in foster care. And while I have moments when I think even a bad foster home might be preferable to this, I still have that old fear. It's hard to get past it. Really, incarceration sounds preferable.

On Friday, Pastor Roland is serving as the on-site counselor at the mission, and I actually made an appointment with him. I have no idea how or if he can help me, but I'm curious about his offer. Was it just empty words? When I walk into his office, he just smiles at me and introduces himself. When I tell him we've already met, he seems confused. Then he looks down at his appointment book. "Adele?" He stands, coming over to look more closely at me. "Is that really you?"

My hand instinctively goes to my face, which is broken out

in an ugly rash. I'm not sure what it's from, but I'm guessing it might be the pillow I've been using. Who knows how many heads have slept on it already? My long hair is pulled back in a greasy ponytail. And my raggedy frumpy clothes are the ones I used to wear only while working at River Woods. I know I look terrible, but I don't really care about things like appearances anymore. Why should I?

"Sit down," he says gently, pulling out the chair for me like I'm a fine lady. "Tell me what's going on."

And because he already knows part of my story, I pour out the second half of my sad, twisted tale. Then I wait for his reaction. But he's just sitting there with his hands folded and a quiet expression on his face, almost as if he's waiting for something.

"And I even visited your church."

"Was that you in the back last Sunday?" His brow creases with concern. "I noticed a stranger, but then she . . . you left."

"Yeah, I didn't really see the point."

"The point?"

"Of being there. I mean, what you were saying sounded nice, but it was a little unreal and out of touch."

"Unreal and out of touch?"

"You know, about how kindness, love, generosity—all that goodness changing the world."

He just nods.

"I mean, I'm sure those qualities exist for *some* people." I attempt a feeble laugh. "Probably the kind of people who don't really need anything in the first place. I'm sure that people with money and friends and homes—they're probably surrounded by love, kindness, and generosity."

"But not you?"

I just shake my head and hope I can keep from crying. I am so sick of tears.

"Can I ask you a question, Adele?"

I shrug. "Sure. Go for it."

"When life was going better for you, when you had more money and a place to live and wealthy friends . . . were you happy?"

"Happy?" I try to wrap my mind around this.

He points to his chest now. "You know, deep inside of you, were you happy, content, fulfilled? Did having those things bring you a sense of happiness?"

"I'm sure I was a lot happier than I am now."

He nods. "But try to remember, did you have a sense of peace inside of you?"

I think about this, then shake my head. "No, I don't think I've ever had a sense of peace inside of me. I've spent most of my life just waiting for the other shoe to fall. Like even if life is good for a while, it won't last. It never does."

He points to one side of the desk. "What if I put a big pile of hundred-dollar bills right here?" Now he points to his Bible. "And what if this represented God?"

I frown. "Huh?"

"And what if I told you to choose one of these, and it would be entirely yours. Which would you choose?"

I try to imagine a really big stack of hundred-dollar bills — it would probably be worth thousands. I know what I could do with money like that: rent an apartment, get some food and some clothes, go back to school. I'm pretty sure I'd choose the cash, but I have a feeling this is a trick question. "Well, because my biggest problem seems to be poverty, and because I don't even know God and I doubt that he cares much about me anyway, I'd probably go with the money."

He nods. "Yes, that's what I thought. But what if I told you

God is worth more than all the money in that pile, and more than all the money in the world? And what if I told you that God can not only provide for you, but he can give you something money can never buy?"

"You mean happiness?"

"Yes . . . and a lot more. If you truly believed that, would you still choose the money?"

I think hard about this. "If what you're saying is true . . . if God really could provide all that I need and give me happiness too . . . well, I'd be a fool to choose the money. It would run out in time anyway."

"Or be stolen like the cash in your flashlight?"

I nod. "Yeah."

"So, what if what I'm telling you is true, Adele?"

"Can you prove it?"

He smiles. "I can prove it by the results in my own life . . . and by the lives of many, many others. But the real proof comes when you allow God to prove it to you himself. That's the only real way to understand what I'm telling you."

"Meaning?" I frown at him.

"Meaning, if you invite God into your life . . . if you open your arms and receive all that he has to offer—his forgiveness and goodness and kindness and mercy—you will begin to understand this for yourself."

I take in a deep breath. "I wish that were true."

"It is true." He smiles. "I challenge you to find out for yourself that it really is true."

"How?" I ask with a shaky voice. I'm still trying to hold back tears. "It sounds impossible . . . and too good to be true."

"For starters, how about if you trust someone to help you?"

I frown. "Trust someone?"

"Yes, I understand you have a hard time trusting, Adele. And I can't say that I blame you for it. The problem is that if you quit trusting everyone, you will always be unhappy."

"But every time I trust someone" — my voice cracks — "they let me down."

"Have I let you down?"

I think about this. "Not yet."

"But you might give up on me before I do let you down, just to make sure that it doesn't happen?"

I just stare at him now. It's like he's reading my mind. "Maybe . . ."

"Help is a two-way street, Adele. Someone must be willing to give . . . someone else must be willing to receive."

I nod eagerly as I remember that fictional pile of money. "Hey, I'm totally willing to receive."

"I'm not just talking about a handout — something you can pocket and take off with. I'm talking about relationships."

"I don't think I understand."

"From what you've told me, you're used to depending on yourself. You're a smart young woman, a hard worker, resourceful, but eventually all those things failed you, right?"

"Yeah."

"In a way, you let yourself down too."

"I guess."

"So maybe it's time to stop relying so much on yourself, Adele. Maybe it's time to rely on others . . . and God, too."

The truth is that actually sounds good to me. Unfortunately, it also sounds too good to be true. "But how? How is that even possible? What do I do?"

"If you're willing to take a chance, I know a very lovely couple who would be happy to open their home to one of God's lost lambs."

Okay, the tears are coming again. "Really?" I don't even feel offended that he called me a lost lamb. In fact, it sounded rather sweet.

He nods. "And their home is within walking distance of your school."

"Really?"

"All you have to do is say yes."

"Yes." I nod eagerly. "Yes!"

With that he picks up the phone, and I listen as he briefly explains my situation. Less than thirty minutes later, a sweet-faced woman named Beth Edwards picks me up at the mission. She seems almost old enough to be my grandmother, yet she has a young look about her. And she chats easily with me as she drives through town.

"I retired early from nursing," she tells me. "And my husband, Jim, has a small accounting firm. Our three children are grown and live away from us, and we have four grandchildren who sometimes come to visit in the summer. So we really do have room in our lives to help someone. And when Pastor Roland told me about you a couple of weeks ago, both Jim and I felt it was the right thing to do."

"Pastor Roland told you about me a couple of weeks ago?"

She pulls into the driveway of a modest but well-kept ranch-style house not four blocks from the high school. "Yes. He was quite taken with you—and the fact that your name was the same as his deceased wife." She turns and smiles at me. "You see, his Adele was a good friend of mine, too."

I'm sure that I'm in a state of shock as she shows me to a bedroom painted the color of a summer sky. "I think you'll like this room. It gets good morning light." Then she gives me the rest of the tour of the neat, comfortable house. "Feel free to use the laundry room to wash your things," she says after she's shown me the sunny yellow room. Finally she stops by a hallway bathroom. "And this will be mostly yours to use, Adele."

I don't even know what to say. "I'm good at keeping things clean," I finally mutter.

She pats me on the shoulder. "I'm sure you are."

"I . . . uh . . . I don't know how to thank you for—"

"You are most welcome, dear. And dinner is at six."

"Can I help you?" I offer.

"Not tonight. For now, I just want you to relax, take a bath or shower, do your laundry, have a nap. I'm sure you've been through a lot."

I nod. "Yeah . . . kind of." Then she goes her way, and although I'm still in a state of shock and wonder, I follow her suggestions to clean up and do laundry, but before I take a nap, I get down on my knees and thank God for giving me this chance.

## Several Months Later

It took me about a week to get over the shock that I actually get to live with Beth and Jim. Pastor Roland was right—they are two of the sweetest people I have ever met. And yet they are not pushy or intrusive. It's like they understand that I still need a little independence, and they give me my space. Even when Beth insisted on taking me shopping for some clothes and things to replace what was stolen, she never tried to press her tastes or styles onto me. And when we finished, she told me I was one of the most sensible teenage shoppers she had ever been privileged to shop with. That was nice.

With some help from Beth, who talked to a school counselor with me, I got back into school and have been able to make up my missed classes by doing extra credit and a few things. And I even admitted to Lindsey, who is now my best friend, that she hadn't been completely wrong about Cybil after all.

"It might've just been pride on my part," I told Lindsey in art shortly after I was back in school. "But at the time I thought I was trying to help Cybil. Unfortunately, she didn't really want my help. It turned out pretty badly."

Lindsey nodded. "I haven't seen Cybil for a couple of weeks. I think she might've moved or something."

Or dropped out. But I wasn't too surprised. Really, that girl just wasn't thinking straight. Even so, I hope Cybil will be okay. And as badly as she wanted her "freedom," I have a feeling it's probably turned into her prison by now . . . one way or another. Speaking of freedom, I admitted to Beth that I am underage. She didn't seem too concerned, and after a few weeks, she set up an appointment with a social worker friend of hers, who actually turned out to be trustworthy. Because my mom is still missing and because I turn eighteen in the spring, they decided no formal report needed to be filed. To say I was greatly relieved is an understatement.

Another thing I was relieved about was Jayden. I honestly didn't think he'd ever speak to me again, but he still wanted to be friends. Or maybe he wanted more, but I told him that just being friends was about all I could handle for now, and he was okay with that.

It took a few weeks, but shortly before Thanksgiving, I returned to River Woods and gave Ms. Michaels a formal apology—telling her the whole truth and nothing but the truth about why I left so abruptly. To my surprise, she seemed to already know all about it. And she told me that some of the residents, especially Mrs. Ashburn, had been asking for me.

Then she offered me my job back, which I gladly accepted. But even before my first day back to work, I visited Mrs. Ashburn. Without going into all the details, I explained to her about my new housing situation, and she seemed very happy for me.

It felt good to be working again, but this time I decided to put in fewer hours. Although I want to earn enough money to cover my personal expenses, as well as to save for college, I don't want my job to take up all my spare time like it did before.

That's partly because I want to have a life, and also because I want some time for volunteering at the mission. I've been helping with the kids' program on Saturdays. It's one of the highlights of my week and something I refuse to give up. Nothing is sweeter than seeing those sad faces transformed into smiles as we play games, do crafts, sing songs, and go to the library for story hour. And the moms appreciate the break too.

Last weekend I nearly fainted when Jayden asked if he could come do it with me. And having him there was great. The kids loved having a guy around, and although Jayden confessed later that he was still trying to wrap his head around this whole homeless thing, he said helping with those kids is changing the way he thinks.

While I wasn't homeless for a long time (even if it felt like an eternity some days), I saw and experienced some things that have forever changed the way I look at homeless people. I used to assume they were lazy or drug addicts or just plain losers. Now I realize that all kinds of people, through all kinds of circumstances, might find themselves without a home at some point in their lives. And I believe it's the job of everyone to help those in need. For that reason, I plan to focus my college education on a degree that will allow me to help others and to make a difference.

Another thing I've learned is that a lot of people are better than I give them credit for. During that time when I felt so alone, I could've gone to Ms. Michaels for help—she even said so. And I could've called on Pastor Roland sooner. And both Lindsey and Jayden told me they would've helped too, but I never gave them the chance. So I guess what Pastor Roland said about giving and receiving is really true—it is a two-way street.

But the most important thing I've learned is that I was wrong—life is not a cosmic coin toss. The whole time I thought I was looking for things like a home, money, friends, food . . . I was really looking for God. I've discovered that knowing God—having a real relationship with him—is worth more than any of the material stuff I thought was missing. And I wouldn't trade my friendship with God for anything. Because like Pastor Roland said, when you get God, you get everything. And that is why I don't think I'll ever be needy again.

1. Adele seemed to be getting a fresh start at the beginning of the story—but then it fell apart. What, if anything, do you think she could've done differently to change the outcome?
2. How do you think the adversity in Adele's life changed her? Did it make her stronger? Weaker? Both?
3. What part of Adele's challenges could you relate to?
4. Describe your initial reaction toward homeless people (like street people or panhandlers). Do you avoid them? Look the other way? Make fun of them? Give them money?
5. What do you think you would do if you suddenly became homeless? Would you try to hide it like Adele did? Who might you turn to for help?
6. Describe your initial reaction to Adele's mother. Did you like her? Trust her? Believe her? Why or why not?
7. What role do you think mental illness played in this story?
8. Do you think Adele had issues with trusting people? Why or why not?
9. Why do you think most people are homeless?
10. What do you think you could do to help homeless people?

MELODY CARLSON has written more than a hundred books for all age groups, but she particularly enjoys writing for teens. Perhaps this is because her own teen years remain so vivid in her memory. After claiming to be an atheist at the ripe old age of twelve, she later surrendered her heart to Jesus and has been following him ever since. Her hope and prayer for all her readers is that each one would be touched by God in a special way through her stories. For more information, please visit Melody's website at www.melodycarlson.com.

# On the Runway
## from Melody Carlson

When Paige and Erin Forrester are offered their own TV show, sisterly bonds are tested as the girls learn that it takes two to keep their once-in-a-lifetime project afloat.

## Premiere
Book One

## Catwalk
Book Two

## Rendezvous
Book Three

## Spotlight
Book Four

*Pick up a copy today at your favorite bookstore!*

**Visit www.zondervan.com/teen**

# MY LIFE IS **TOUGHER** THAN MOST **PEOPLE REALIZE.**

I TRY TO
KEEP EVERYTHING
IN BALANCE:
FRIENDS. FAMILY. WORK.
SCHOOL. AND GOD.

IT'S NOT EASY.

I KNOW WHAT MY
PARENTS BELIEVE AND
WHAT MY PASTOR SAYS.

BUT IT'S NOT
ABOUT THEM.
IT'S ABOUT ME...

ISN'T IT TIME I
OWN MY FAITH?

THROUGH THICK AND THIN, KEEP YOUR HEARTS AT ATTENTION, IN
ADORATION BEFORE CHRIST, YOUR MASTER. BE READY TO SPEAK
UP AND TELL ANYONE WHO ASKS WHY YOU'RE LIVING THE WAY
YOU ARE, AND ALWAYS WITH THE UTMOST COURESY. 1 PETER 3:15

www.navpress.com | 1-800-366-7788     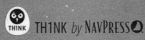 THINK  TH1NK by NAVPRESS